Alligator Crossing

Alligator Crossing

MARJORY STONEMAN DOUGLAS

Illustrations by Trudy Nicholson

MILKWEED
EDITIONS

The characters and events in this book are fictitious. Any similarity to real persons, living or dead, is coincidental and not intended by the author.

Published 2003 by Milkweed Editions
Printed in Canada
Jacket and interior design by Christian Fünfhausen
Jacket and interior art by Trudy Nicholson
Author photo on jacket flap courtesy of Florida Photographic Collection
   Florida State Archive
The text of this book is set in New Baskerville.
03 04 05 06 07   5 4 3 2 1
Originally published by the John Day Company, 1959.

Special underwriting for this book was provided by Furthermore, a program of the J.M. Kaplan Fund.

Milkweed Editions, a nonprofit publisher, gratefully acknowledges support from the Bush Foundation; Joe B. Foster Family Foundation; General Mills Foundation; Jerome Foundation; Dorothy Kaplan Light; Lila Wallace-Reader's Digest Fund; Marshall Field's Project Imagine with support from the Target Foundation; McKnight Foundation; Minnesota State Arts Board through an appropriation by the Minnesota State Legislature; National Endowment for the Arts; Kate and Stuart Nielson; Deborah Reynolds; St. Paul Companies, Inc.; Ellen and Sheldon Sturgis; Surdna Foundation; Target Foundation; Gertrude Sexton Thompson Charitable Trust; James R. Thorpe Foundation; Toro Foundation; United Arts Fund of COMPAS; Lois Ream Waldref; Brenda Wehle and John C. Lynch; and Xcel Energy Foundation

Library of Congress Cataloging-in-Publication Data

Douglas, Marjory Stoneman.
   Alligator crossing / Marjory Stoneman Douglas ; illustrations by Trudy Nicholson. — 1st ed.
      p. cm.
   Summary: Fleeing bullies and life with his stepfamily, Henry Bunks finds a secret hideaway that becomes his observation point for activities in the Florida Everglades, legal and otherwise.
   ISBN 1-57131-640-X (hardcover : alk. paper) —
ISBN 1-57131-644-2 (pbk. : alk. paper)
   [1. Everglades (Fla.)—Fiction. 2. Florida—Fiction. 3. Bullies—Fiction. 4. Crocodiles—Fiction. 5. Poaching—Fiction.]   I. Nicholson, Trudy H., ill. II. Title.
PZ7.D7474AI 2003
[Fic]—dc21

                                                                  2002151110

To Barney Parker
Devoted Everglades Ranger

Alligator Crossing

1. The loose board in the fence
2. Down the Miami River
3. Bay of Florida
4. Madeira Bay
5. Flamingo
6. Open Gulf Water
7. Cape Sable by Moonlight
8. Beyond Whitewater Bay
9. Alligator Crossing
10. Pond full of Gators
11. The Labyrinth
12. To Lostman's River
13. Man Hunt
14. End of the Search

Miami R.

1 & 2
MIAMI
41

27
1

HOMESTEAD
TEMP.
PARK
H.Q.
FLORIDA
CITY

ROYAL
PALM
STA.
RM. PARK H.Q.
1

ATLANTIC OCEAN

Bay

EVERGLADES
NATIONAL PARK
Scene of Alligator Crossing

*Names of events and locations
connected with the Story are
shown in italics: Man Hunt*
🌓 *Ranger Station*
🔺 *Fire Lookout*
→ → → — — → *Route of Motor Boat*

Alligator Crossing

The Loose Board in the Fence

HENRY'S bony legs ached with keeping ahead of the seven pairs of feet pounding relentlessly behind. His throat ached. His chest ached. He knew how the boys grinned like dogs. But if he could just keep his legs going around the corner ahead, there was the loose board in the fence.

"Bunk, you little rat, wait—we got something for you," they shouted, laughing and catcalling. He could not run another step. Yet he ran harder. The fence corner was at his hand. He turned it, flung himself head first under the bushes, hit the board. It swung. He was through.

Seven pairs of feet went thudding by outside. The big

boys yelped down the alley that turned into a dead end, where they thought they had him at last to themselves. But within there, Henry was dancing silently a gleeful dance of escape and derision, all to himself, with legs that felt fine. All to himself in a weedy yard, among empty barrels and boxes, he tossed his arms and legs in wild gestures of triumph, twisting his face in silent shoutings, threatening soundlessly to throw the rock he had picked up, to heave it at any head that might look over the fence. He was still panting, but now it was with relief and excitement and pride in his own strength and cunning.

But he caught himself up prudently. They were yelling in wrath down by the alley's end and they might be back, poking about among the bushes. So he dropped the rock and trotted away on the winding trail he had discovered for himself, to the secret place, safe and hidden, that more than any other in the world was his own.

He flipped around a shed, through a hedge, under a wire fence, and dodged among the rotting lumber of an old boatyard, giggling under his breath. He couldn't help it. He made himself slow up and stop grinning as he strolled down past the little house, in case the old woman looked out. Before, he had politely taken off his cap to her and politely asked her permission. "I am Henry Albert Bunks," he had said. "Please may I look for a lost boat?" Maybe she had been too deaf to hear him, but she had nodded.

Nobody saw him now, in the hot Florida midday sun

that blasted the green bushes and the huddle of roofs among lots filled with tin cans and weeds.

At the end of the path he ducked under another wire into rank weeds taller than his head, following his own secret trail. Beyond the high bank, brown canal water rippled with wind, dark green under the shadowy wall of Australian pines beyond. He slipped in a shower of stones down the bank to the water and then crawled downstream, one foot in mud, under the bank higher than his head. He climbed over the planks of the old boat half out of water. The bank was thick with bushes. Then it opened back in a gully. Several feet up under a weedy overhang there was a dark hole.

In there he could almost stand upright, breathing happily the cool smell of earth, staring out at the hot sunshine sparkling on the water where the gully ended in a shelflike beach and a rock. It was all his.

He had moved the fallen rocks so that his floor was level underfoot and piled them up in a half wall against the opening, a wall that he could hide behind. He turned and touched the holes he had made in the bank. His things were all safe—the jar of matches, the tin can of his favorite pebbles, the old fishing line and rusty fish hook, and his special treasure, the broken knife he had sharpened on a rock. They were just as he had left them.

He took off his wet shirt, kicked away his old sneakers and the worn shorts his mother had not patched, down to his faded swim trunks. His body, but for his brown arms and legs, still looked white and weedy in this green half-light. "Small for his age," everybody always said, turning indifferently away from the face that maddened him, also, because it didn't look like any special face at all—just a thin nose and eyes no particular color and freckles in odd places and pale tan hair like a wirehaired dog's. In that crowded place where he lived it seemed to him that nobody looked at him, or if they did, they didn't see him. Sometimes that was an advantage but more times it made him lonely. But not here. None of that mattered here. Here he was Henry Albert Bunks, bigger and taller and stronger and more important every minute. Here the name, which was all his father had left him, sounded as if it meant something, almost as much as he wanted it to.

He ducked out the hole and felt the warm rocky earth under his feet and the air like cool silk on his delighted skin. The wind rippled the dark trees opposite with a swishy sighing. Canal water flowed by quietly, smacked from time to time by little jumping fish. A blue jay screamed. All around him, in comfort, lay the sunny silence.

The city streets from which he had escaped were only a dull murmur far away. Far away was the place he lived— the narrow noisy room crowded with younger children that were nothing to him except that they belonged to his mother and his stepfather. There was nothing about them like the brothers and sisters he had once imagined he would have. Even his mother, who had become such a different, almost an unknown, person because of all these things, was far back there—too far to brood over.

He stood tall and breathed deep and slowly looked around him at his world, letting his mind enjoy the difference between what lay behind him and this. He relished the cool air and the cool water more because it was not the hot shadeless sidewalk by the big masonry apartment house where he and too many other people lived, where there was only the sidewalk to play on for all the children and the big boys, and where there were the chalked games and the spent balls and the crying and shouting within the street, which flowed with the roaring traffic of cars and trucks like a clanking metal river.

There was no room there for anybody, any child, to have anything of his own that would not be snatched from him, or to be anything except what they all were— pushing and screaming children. Now in vacation time there was not even school to go to in crowds of children his own size, which made it fairly safe if you didn't have to stay after school and come home by yourself. Sometimes he liked school, especially when the teacher read stories about birds and animals in some far country where there was room to run about or to sit still in and listen—like this.

Vacation could be worse than just having somebody push you against a wall and take your cookie, if you had a cookie. There were too many big boys standing about idle or ranging the streets in packs. Once they had made him stand "chickie" for them because he was small and inconspicuous, watching at the corner for the cop while they stole bananas from the vegetable man's wagon. It had scared him so he could never walk by the traffic policeman without going all over gooseflesh.

If he tried to get away from the apartment where the children cried and his mother quarreled or from the bare glaring streets where the piles of trash and overflowing garbage cans wait for the city pickup trucks, there was the danger of some bigger gang of boys catching him in territory beyond that they called their own— a region of junkyards and old stores and broken frame houses. The children knew well what happened to boys that the gangs caught there. You couldn't tell it to the policemen, either, or to any grown-up.

It had taken a lot of willpower to make him want to get away from all that. He knew the risk he ran. Maybe he would have been happy enough to have tagged along with the gang from his block and tried to do what they did and what the big boys told them, helping them steal things and thinking up crazy things to do that would make them think he was somebody to admire. Maybe— if he had not remembered the river.

Once when he was little and his father was alive, they had gone walking under green trees. There was a grassy park he remembered and beyond, the gleam and shine of water running, with white boats on it that he and his father had stopped and watched. And under white clouds there were big birds diving into it, plunging down, splashing, and bursting up with the water drops spraying and maybe with a fish in their beaks. Pelicans, his father had told him. They could watch them floating with their great bills tucked into their whity gray feathers, like big old fat men with little wise eyes. His father had fished from a little bridge and let him hold the line and feel the water tugging at it, and once, while his hand was still on it, a fish had pulled at it, as big as the bird's. His father had brought the fish up, curving and flipping water in his own face. They had taken it home and had it for supper. That was a different house then. He had remembered forever, it seemed to him, the wind over the water and the little waves glittering in the sunshine. He had thought of it like that often as he was going off to sleep.

It was after that that everything had changed in his world. Sometimes it seemed to him there was no place where he wanted to belong or to be. His father was nowhere. His mother married this big man with the heavy eyebrows and the beery breath. They lived in the crowded place. But he always remembered the river. To think of it was like being very hungry or thirsty. He couldn't stop wanting it. So in spite of the fear of the big boys, he had gone poking about looking for it, glancing down streets on his way to school, going wandering with five or six other boys of his age, or ranging farther when he dared to, perhaps dodging back on the heels of a group of home-going men.

Then once, he had stayed out of school and found the alley and the loose board and stuck his head through. Beyond there, at last he had found the canal. It had made everything different—until today, when he had been seen.

Now he sat down on his rock and cooled his hot feet in the water. Everything was all right now. Everything was perfect, except that after a while he would have to figure out another way to go back or they'd certainly catch him. They'd be waiting and dodging about watching for him, furious at the way he had disappeared right out of their clutches. They'd be wild until they figured out how he had done it, and got their hands on him. It was scary to think of.

But now he didn't care. He almost laughed aloud, thinking of their faces. If he could only have seen them. For a while at least, it proved he was smarter than they were.

All you had to do, he began to think, was keep on being smarter. They were not awfully smart, either. Some of the biggest of them were stupid. They were a bunch of big muscle-bound toughs with thick heads. Some of them couldn't even spell "cat." He expanded now in the reassurance of his own superior smartness that had surely brought him here. Pretty soon he would think of something smarter yet, smarter than anybody had ever thought of, that would get him back safe again. Pretty soon he would begin to think. Now it was enough just to sit and be here, grinning a little.

How wonderful if he could just stay right here and never go back at all. He fell into a long happy imagining, thinking how he would live on fish he caught, sleep when he wanted to, explore along the canal bank as far as he wanted to, following the canal down to the river. Perhaps a drifting boat would come by and he would get in and float in it down the river, down under the bridges. He was happy in the sun, half-staring at the rippling water, taking deep easy breaths.

There was nothing here but quiet. Upstream he was hidden by the old rotting boat. Across the canal, beyond the plushy green wall of trees where some black birds with red shoulders chirped and chirred, there was the dense green of some old grove. Once in a while an old man came and fished silently there, sitting in a broken chair, noticing nothing. Downstream, under high weed-grown banks, there were old boats tied up, houseboats like shanties, with a few men tinkering about them. He had no idea where the canal water came from. Down there a long way, he thought vaguely, it must flow into the wider river. He daydreamed about that, that he would find an empty boat floating that would carry him down past boats, under bridges, through the glittering noisy city, out to the bay, maybe even to the sea. He could not imagine what it would be like. But his boat would take him there and he would never come back.

He turned his head slowly, making his dazed eyes focus. Maybe he could beg some bait off the woman in the faded blue houseboat who had once given him a cookie. Now he saw that a different boat was tied there to the bank. It was a big, scarred, sun-bleached, gray cabin cruiser. There was a wooden awning over the

cockpit. He read on the stern TRIXIE, MARCO, FLORIDA.
There was no one on her that he could see. He sat and
thought vaguely that it must be a long way from here
in Miami around to wherever Marco was, maybe to the
Florida west coast. He remembered a school map he had
been shown of this country; he wished now that he had
really studied it.

By and by he scrambled up the bank to where he
could look down into the bare cockpit. There was a lock
on the cabin doors. He went back to sitting on his rock,
letting the glint of sun on the brown water, the feel of
the wind on his skin, the sound of birds, the quiet, the
safeness, the aloneness, sink into all the places that had
ached.

He had almost forgotten the fish head he had
brought for George. He had rolled it up in paper and
thrust it into his shirt along with the potato he had
snitched from the grocery store. He would build a fire
and boil the potato by and by, if he couldn't catch a
fish—after George had come.

He put the fish head on the flat rock just at the
water's edge below his own rock, so that its rich pervad-
ing smell could creep out across the brown ripples to
the other bank, where the tall reeds were and where
George had some kind of a muddy hole or cave of his
own. Henry sat back and waited. New warmth flooded
up him—the sense he had found here before of release
and gladness.

It did not matter now how long he waited. His mouth

twitched with a smile as he heard the little ripple coming. When he turned his head gently a knobby stick was floating slantwise across the canal, coming straight to him. Anybody else would have thought it was a stick. Henry knew better.

A small dark knob or knot moved ahead in a widening V-shaped ripple. About a foot behind that, two dark bumps were blinking eyes, watching him fixedly, just out of the water. Behind that was a swirling about two feet long, finished off by a gently moving dark ridge. That was George's tail.

A current might have been carrying him, he came with such ease. When he was nearer, Henry could see the rounded outline of his long nose, a broad shadow just underwater. Behind the broad jaws he saw the two front legs trailing idly like round, bowed arms with fat hands and pointed fingers. His fat body with all its knobs and ridges moved under the dimpling water. His fat hind legs trailed. It was the easy sculling of his ridgy tail that kept him gliding so smoothly. Henry could see how one really powerful swish of that tail could send him charging down the canal like a surfaced submarine.

Henry could not keep himself from grinning, even with his mouth closed, as he made the little grunting squeals in the back of his throat, which he had learned from the old man across the way was the accepted method of calling an alligator out of his muddy, reedy hole.

Now George grounded himself as gently as any drifting stick on the pebbly slope of the bank below Henry's

feet. He lifted his whole head out of water on his fat
bowed forelegs. His fat black body came up. Henry sat
breathless with delight. The water ran off among the
knobs and ridges of the wet dark head and back. Under
their thick hoods George's round eyes with their slitted
pupils watched him. It seemed to the motionless boy
that the eyes knew him, that the long curling mouth,
where the jaws came together like the closing of a
satchel, smiled at him.

George wasn't very long—about three feet from the
bumps on the end of his nose that were his alert nostrils,
down his leathery, buttony, scaly back to his tail. There
was mud on him. He was clumsy on his bowed legs when
he lifted up and hitched forward until his nostrils lay by
the fish head. But there was something queer and wise
and old about him. It seemed as if he knew everything
and had lived through everything, as though he were
out of some other world. But here he was, utterly at ease,
unafraid, and certainly not frightening, less than a foot
from the boy's foot. The eyes seemed to be watching
him in confidence and in friendship.

The boy began to feel that he really was Henry
Albert Bunks, strong and sure, bigger, more important.
The warm heady happy thing rising in him was pride.
Certainly there was no one he knew exactly like him, who
had found out such a place as his here and had risked
everything for it; no other boy he had ever heard of had
his own alligator.

The water rippled. The sun moved a little. In the

shadow of the trees the little fish woke and jumped for drowsy insects. George moved a little and opened his prodigious jaw to nip at the fish head, shake it, and take it down with him into the water to gulp it. Then he came back gently to rest his long chin on the rock and let his hind legs and his ridgy tail swing in the little current.

Henry bustled around happily, lighting his crackling little fire of sticks, boiling his potato in an old can, digging out from its hole his little jar of salt. When the potato was cool enough to peel and eat, it seemed to him it was better than anything he had ever tasted. He tossed the potato skins into the water and watched two little fish nibble at them. Then he got out the piece of fish skin he had saved and sat dangling his line from another rock that jutted into the canal.

Once in a while a big white gull flew over or a glossy black crow cawed at him. Once George slipped away and sculled upstream and came back again, chonking on what seemed like all that was left of a small turtle. Then he shoved up higher, in a curve on the warm bank, and seemed to go to sleep, and Henry, who hadn't caught anything yet, jiggled his line and half dozed, forgetting to be anything but happy.

He was startled awake by a shadow lengthening over him. A tall skinny dark-haired man stood there above him, in blue jeans and a stained shirt blowing over a hollow chest. A ratty, wide-brimmed straw hat that was pitched over his nose cut its shadow across his face, in which his eyes gleamed white-blue, with whitish lashes.

He had a peculiar grin. His lip seemed to curl away from strong yellow teeth. But he was not looking at Henry. His glance went straight to George the alligator, half curled on the rocky sand. "Bout three foot," he said. He glanced across the canal at the empty chair where the old man sometimes sat. "Where's his hole?" he asked.

His eyes glinted to the place where Henry pointed. He threw away the cigarette in his fingers and turned, saying nothing more, walked back under the bank to that gray fish boat. He had things to lift on board, a kerosene can and a glass demijohn of water and bags of groceries. He swung himself neatly over into the cockpit. Henry heard only a few sounds he made after that, stowing away his things.

Once when Henry got up and stretched and turned to look that way, he saw the man sitting quietly doing something with his hands, whittling or polishing something, now and then turning his head to glance back where Henry was. Even at that distance, Henry could see the man's lip curl away from his teeth, with his eyes in shadow.

The sun was lower in the west than it had been, shining yellow, straight down the straightness of the canal within the green line of trees, making the brown water look dusty. An open boat with an outboard went up, trailing its bow wave along with it, drawing a line of foamy water high along the bank. When it was quiet again, Henry saw that George had slipped away.

The afternoon was over. It would be dark too soon. Slowly, Henry remembered his dread. He rolled up his wet string and climbed up to his hole to put it away, along with his cooking can and his jar of salt. He put on his shorts and his shirt and slowly tied on his old worn sneakers. Everything he did now made him feel smaller and more insignificant because he knew that he did not dare to stay here any longer. He would be hungry. The earth and rocks were a worse place to sleep than the cot he shared with his three-year-old half brother, who wet the bed. He felt the curious dragging helplessness of a child who must do what he hates and fears doing because he can't think of anything else.

He could not go home by the same way he had come. He could not be sure that they were not still watching for him.

He walked slowly past the big gray boat. The man was just coming up out of his cabin in a mussed tan suit with a black hat over his eyes. He went to the boat's side and pulled on the painter of his dinghy.

"Mister," Henry said hurriedly, "are you going to town in your boat?"

The man grudged him a nod. "Down to the Twelfth Avenue Bridge," he said.

"Let me go with you? I got to get home."

It was clear the man did not want to bother with him, but the sudden white intensity in Henry's face held his eye. "Scared," he said. It was not a question. There was contempt in it. As soon as he nodded, Henry was in the boat. Elation twisted his mouth but he sat rigid, watching the bank flow by.

Before they got to the bridge, the man turned the bow into a boatyard cove. "Look," he said, "run over to the drugstore across the street. Get me two packs of cigarettes and a box of rubber nipples, and hurry."

Henry stared at him in surprise. "You got a baby?" He certainly didn't seem like a man who had a baby.

"Don't ask silly questions," he snapped. "Get going."

Henry trotted along as fast as he could. At the street there was the traffic banging and honking and swishing the same as ever, dusty and glittering, endless so long as the light did not turn. The light turned. He ran across. Now all the delight of his day lay hidden within him, a treasure to be taken out and studied later. But not now. This was it—the time when he had to be smart to get home safe. It was a long walk home and it would be dark and dangerous, the time for big boys to be prowling. There was nothing smart that he could think of.

He bought the cigarettes. He walked to the back of the store to buy the nipples. He knew exactly the sort of counter. He had bought dozens. He waited on the corner again for the green light, jingling the change, trying hard to think. He could think of nothing.

Traffic sighed to a stop. He darted across under the green, jogged through the boatyard, found his man, frowning and impatient in the cockpit, who snatched the things out of Henry's hand, counted his change twice and gave Henry a nickel.

"A nickel, a nickel, a nickel," Henry said to himself, "what can you do with a nickel!" He stood on the dock to watch the boat push off, start up, go thundering back up to the canal. When that was gone he was alone.

He stood on the corner in front of the drugstore again, his hand sweaty on the nickel in his pocket. Perhaps it was better than nothing but he could not think why. His head followed every grinding roar of every truck going his way. He would be so safe and happy in any high cab, going fast in the right direction, safely carried above all that metal tide. But not a single driver turned his head to look at him as he stood, feeling smaller and smaller. People went by, bumping him. He hopped on and off the curb, waving his thumb more and more frantically. Nobody saw him.

Something chinked on the stone. He looked down. It was his nickel, rolling. It must have stuck to his hand when he brought it out of his pocket to wave. It rolled into the street and Henry dived after it. After all, it was his nickel.

Brakes screamed. Traffic bells shrilled. A man shouted and cursed. Henry got his hand on his nickel right under the wheel of a truck that had ground to a stop just by the curb.

The man in the cab banged open the door and glared down at Henry, yelling, "What you mean, you little devil, scaring me to death? Lucky you ain't dead. Lucky you ain't—"

Henry looked up into the broad, red, furious face.

"Hey, Mr. Hennessey, hey," he shouted. "My nickel. Look. I got it. Look, Mr. Hennessey." He crowded up to the step, holding up his nickel in his dirty hand.

The man yelled, "Get away—get off—the light's turning—what's the matter with you anyway?"

"Mr. Hennessey, Mr. Hennessey!" Henry shouted, leaping up on the step. "Look, I—"

The man leaned and grabbed Henry by the collar and dragged him up. "Get in here then—my gosh—you crazy—the light . . ."

The truck roared forward as the traffic leaped and Henry sat up on the high seat, grinning and babbling, "Mr. Hennessey, thank you Mr. Hennessey."

The man said, "My name ain't Hennessey."

"I can see it isn't, Henry said happily. "I can see now you're a lot bigger and stronger than Mr. Hennessey and your truck's bigger. I can see it's about the biggest truck in the world—so I'll be glad to pay you my nickel if you're going up Seventh Avenue to my street—which is where Mr. Hennessey would be glad to go anytime because his boy is a good friend of mine and about the smartest boy I know, only he wouldn't always take my nickel—and it's a long walk home and getting darker."

The truck driver took a long look at Henry who was sticking his freckled nose out of the cab window, with his hair blowing back in the wind, blinking and grinning like a little dog. High among the traffic, the truck sailed and Henry was borne on it as if it were a pink cloud.

"Aw, come off it," the truck driver shouted at him.

"You don't know any Hennessey and he hasn't got any boy and you know darn well you can keep your nickel, and for scaring me to death I'll prob'ly drive you right up to your house and get out and open the cab door for you with my hat off, Mr. Smartypants."

"Maybe I am," Henry shouted at him laughing, "but still I'm not as smart as you are and I know it."

The big truck took him right up to his own corner. But before Henry got down he'd learned that the man's name was really McGonigle and he had two twin little girls and a boy baby and a puppy and a parrot and his wife had red hair. So Henry said, just before he got down, "Mr. McGonigle, you wouldn't be going back again down toward the river sometime before daylight and you wouldn't be willing to stop and pick me up and let me ride as far as the bridge over the canal, would you, because I've got some very important business up the canal as early as I can get there?"

Mr. McGonigle burst into a big shout of laughter in which his eyes wrinkled up tight in his broad red face, "By gorry and I would, Mr. Smartpants, if on'y to have the pleasure of your company in the cold gray dawn of day, because it's then I'll be comin' down the cross street, on'y you got to be standin' down there by the fillin' station at exactly on the dot of four-thirty, no more, no less. An' you'll know it's me in the biggest truck in the world because you can see for yourself the large sign on my windshield that says, 'No Riders.'"

Down the Miami River

THAT night Henry did not mind going to bed early in the frowsy back room, where the children were packed in, three in one bed and he with the three-year-old in the hottest corner. Traffic noises from the street below, the sounds of feet trampling in the hall, and TV sets shouting and thumping did not distract him now. At regular intervals the refrigerator door slammed. Bottle caps popped. His mother coughed in the front room. He was oblivious.

All he could think of was Mr. McGonigle, and his truck, and waiting on the corner, and the bridge that crossed the canal much lower down. He could work his way up along the bank to his cave. No boys would see him go. If it were a mile or two, it would not matter. Such a new spirit of daring rose in his heart that he almost did not sleep at all.

When he woke it was late at night. The city streets were almost still. In the next room his stepfather was snoring. Henry slipped out of bed. In the glare of the street light the kitchen clock showed four fifteen. In fifteen minutes the truckman would go by the corner.

He had lain down in his shirt and shorts. Now, carrying his sneakers, he poked carefully about the kitchen for something to eat later. He could not risk the noise of the refrigerator door, but he found a loaf of bread, an opened can of beans, and two raw potatoes. The lock on the apartment door, as he tried it, sounded like a shot. His stepfather stopped snoring. He turned over and said something. Henry clung to the door. If the man's stinging hand stopped him he didn't know what he could do. The man's grumbling voice ceased. The floor did not creak. The noise of a truck going by covered Henry's desperate attack on the lock. The door opened. His racing bare feet made no sound along the stuffy hall, or downstairs. Outside he did not stop to put on his sneakers, running along the night-cooled dew-wet pavement.

On the corner he stood in an agony of hope full in the light of the trucks that glared up to him and past. Overhead the stars were shining bits of tin. He trembled with excitement and fear and yet, under the lumpy things he held tight to his thin chest, he was breathing deep into him, as if his very heart were hollow, the sweetness and freshness of the thinning night.

Lights blinded him and stopped. It was Mr. McGonigle shouting at him, grinning as Henry scrambled up into the high cab, nearly spilling the beans. The great truck's lurch and roar was power and safety and delight.

It was a little lighter when the truck left him by the bridge where the canal flowed into the greater river. He began his long, difficult, scrambling expedition westward under the bank, along the bank, around boats, under fences, bushes, wires, over broken automobiles and piles of cast-off junk. Once a dog chased him. When he got beyond another fence to the water's edge again, beans jolted from the opened can were trickling down his panting chest. He scraped them off and ate them thoughtfully from his sticky fingers. They made him feel better. He had no idea how much farther it would be as he went on.

The sky overhead was clear light blue. The first sunlight touched the tops of the highest trees and the gilded birds wheeling beyond them, but the canal water below was still dim in a kind of brown twilight with mists curling up against the green shadowed trees. The houseboats he trudged past, ducking under their lines, were still shut for the night and silent. It was a very strange world to him until a boat with an outboard motor went grandly rushing past him, its bow wave yellow glass and white foam. The man in the stern waved at Henry. As he stood to wave back, he felt they were joined in the pride of being the only people in the clean shine of the early world.

The cool air began to be streaked with warmth as the sun lay its heat on steaming roofs and wet planks. The going was no easier but he made steady progress. Now in his hot face his eyes stung with sleep. There was no excitement left, only doggedness. It seemed as if he had come miles.

Then, with relief, he began to recognize things he had passed so swiftly in the boat yesterday—the old boatyard where the leveled bank was spongy with rotting chips, a half-fallen-in plank walk, tied-up boats. There was the blue houseboat, bright in the sun, with a wonderful smell of bacon cooking. There was the big gray fishboat, locked and still, as if the man were still asleep in it. He saw with a tremendous sense of homecoming his own rock and his own gullied bank and his door hole, shadowy, halfway up it. He had time only to glance back at the familiar brown water with a slow tide beginning to push up, and the wind ruffling the green needles of Australian pines opposite. Then he lay down in safety on the cool rocks within his wall, put his head on a bundle he made of his shirt and the bread and his swim trunks, and eased himself down into sleep.

When he woke the light outside was bright with noon. He went down to cool his sticky body in the water, daring to take only a few swimming strokes and coming out ravenous for his beans and bread, looking around him with new eyes. He did not admit to himself the possibility that before dark, he would have to go back. He was too happy here. The tide was creeping out. He got his hook and string and baited it with a lump of bread. It was time George was coming over.

Grass stems went by slowly, beetles, a piece of board. No fish jumped. He did not notice the city's sounds or the hammering from a distant boatyard. He kept looking over for George, calling to him with those throaty 'gator sounds that he always heeded. There was no George.

Of course, he might have gone upstream hunting. Henry pushed that way along the bank, beyond the bush. By the old boat, something was floating, a lump of brown and white. He started to poke it with a stick. A limp claw showed, a stripped dead tail floated sluggishly, half underwater. He looked at it with such horror that he could not think clearly. It was what was left of George. He had been killed and skinned, from under his lower jaw down his belly to the tip of his tail.

Henry went back and huddled up on his rock, sick to his stomach. His eyes smarted. But he could not cry. He could not look at the water until the lump of stuff had floated by on the outgoing tide. Even then he could hardly move. Somebody had killed George. His alligator. It took time to quiet the jerks in his stomach. The best thing he had ever had. He turned his head slowly, looking here and there as if he could convince himself that it was not true.

He was staring dully at a long drying streak of red

over the stern boards of that fishboat swinging a little on its lines. It meant nothing to him at first. Then he remembered the face of that man there, with his eyes narrowed, looking at the alligator on the bank. He saw exactly what must have happened.

Henry stood up slowly. He was hot. He was shivering. He did not know how he felt except that he was eaten up with anger. Nothing in his life had prepared him for the power of his anger now.

He walked quickly along the bank to the boat, pulled it nearer by the stern line. The cockpit was bare and clean. The stain inside had been washed away. The cabin doors were still locked. He said, "Anybody there?" in a croaking voice that was not his. There was no one. He ran back to his cave and got his sharpened short knife, picked up a rock. His feet made no sound as he jumped over into the boat.

It took him five minutes to hammer and pry open the lock. When he slipped down the ladderlike steps within, the doors swung to behind him. There was light enough through the screened portholes to see the heaps of things within there, things on two bunks with canvass mattresses. He stood and peered here and there among the things, fish lines, hook boxes, clothes hanging up, a water bottle, a rifle in the corner. He stooped and looked at it curiously. There was a new rubber nipple over the end, with a hole shot through it. There were cupboards over the bunks, under the bunks. There was a small dirty oil stove and a little sink in a kind of compartment by the door, frying pan, coffee pot, broken spoons, cans of stuff, a box with bread, a small icebox, filled.

Forward there was another cupboard door, opening into a smelly space within the bow, filled with old gear. The first thing he saw was a rolled-up strip of alligator hide, salted, tied with string. He touched the knobs on each side, the square-sided leathery plates that he had never touched before. He stood over it, empty now of everything but misery. He was only a small-sized boy who knew well his own helplessness. Life was grimmer than he had ever known. His stomach heaved. His eyes stung. In another minute he would have been sobbing.

But from up the canal bank by his rock he heard suddenly a lot of screaming laughter, catcalling, familiar yelling. He put his eye to the crack between the cabin doors. Pouring down his bank, dancing on his rock, he saw the blue jeans and flapping shirts of those big boys he had almost forgotten. They must have found the loose board in the fence and the way to the canal bank. They found his hole, his shirt, his shorts, the rest of his bread. His potatoes, his can of beans, went splash into the water. They snatched at his shirt and tore it to bits and left them in the water. They brought out his hoarded shells and ground them to powder. Then they ran up the bank and began jumping down into the gully, tearing down the roots and dirt and weedy grass that had made his roof, kicking out his wall of stones, scattering and demolishing everything. Under his eyes, it became only a slide of dirt and meaningless heaps of rocks.

They were staring around them, moving along now in a silent huddle, mouths grinning in the varied shapes of their faces. Tall boys, fat boys, brown boys, eyes alike, mouths alike, eager and hard and ruthless, looking for the next thing to hurt or smash.

The leader sneaked up to the fishboat. They huddled behind him listening and waiting, peering into the cockpit. Henry was afraid they would see the doors tremble in his hands. He drew back into the shadows of the cabin. The rifle was there, just beyond his hand. If it were loaded, would he dare use it? He heard the thud of feet on the cockpit boards.

Then from the bank above a man shouted. The boys laughed under their breaths. One catcalled. Their feet scrambled back along the bank. He heard the man swear at them. They must have disappeared up the bank, throwing a few careless stones.

The man stepped into his cockpit. He dropped something heavy on the boards, moved a pail, walked to the doors and swore again, stooping to look at the broken lock.

Henry had already begun to feel his way backward as silently as he could, among all the clutter of things. The man was swearing and fingering the lock as Henry found the knob of that cupboard or locker within the very shape of the bow and threw himself in on stinking canvas, in almost unbreathable heat. He drew the door shut just before the flare of light from the opened doors fell into the cabin.

The man must have stood peering into the dimness with dazzled eyes for what might have been smashed or stolen. The butt of the light gun grated. Then he must have relaxed, seeing nothing lost. But to Henry, huddled up in the musty dark forward, corners of things sticking into his heaving ribs, one foot on the roll of salted alligator hide, the man in the cabin was only listening for him to move or make a sound.

Henry's arm went to sleep and stung, his knees ached with being curled up, his back was sore. He could hardly breathe. Sweat trickled in salty streams down his face, tickled his nose, ran into his panting mouth. The man banged around the cabin up and down the steps, bringing things down from the cockpit. Henry lay rigid.

Then for what seemed like another hour the man was busy on the deck. It sounded as if he had taken up boards and was working on the engine. Under the covering noise Henry uncramped his legs, dared to crawl to the locker door and set it a crack ajar so that he could lie and breathe. Once or twice when the man's footsteps thudded on the deck overhead he opened it wide, stared, breathed hard, and closed it again but for the crack.

He had not the slightest idea what he could do. His mind was numbed. From time to time a flush of that rage he had felt surged up in him. If the man found him here, he might kill him. His only hope was to be able to stay here until the man went off again, and then run for it—downstream.

Through the locker door and the open cabin doors it seemed to him the sun was yellow in the west. A little cooler air came through. He dared to move, cautiously rubbing a stinging knee or a cramped arm. The sudden, violent, astounding roar of the engine was like a blow in his face. Through the crack, one of Henry's eyes at a time could just make out the man's head and shoulders up there in the cockpit, at a long tiller. The engine roared gently. The whole boat throbbed. There was a grating alongside. The man was bending and pushing. It was a minute or two before Henry really believed that the rushing sounds beyond the boards where he lay meant moving water, that the boat, slowly, with an idling engine, was drawing out to the middle of the canal, going downstream. Presently the roar deepened. The whole bow lifted. Water slapped below.

Henry began to breathe fresh salt air coming through his crack. The boat jarred under him, bounced and rushed. He was swallowed up in the roaring and rushing—down the canal, under the clanging bells of bridges. He lay helpless as a joggled log, afraid, assaulted, amazed. The boat curved and rushed in deeper water. Was it the river? Were those the hooting horns of other boats? The boat rushed faster in the rushing silence of wide water, going fast, going out—where?

The Bay of Florida

T HERE came a moment when Henry's excitement, bewilderment, and fear became complete exhaustion and he slept. But huddled anyhow among lumpy and sharp-edged things, his sleep was miserable in the bouncing, roaring dark and confused with dreams.

He woke suddenly to silence and a comfortable rocking of boards under him. Water slapped and sloshed below his ear. He held his breath to listen for other sounds beyond the creaking door. He could hear nothing else. He was most aware now of his body's acute discomfort. His mouth was dry as cotton. He was thirsty and starved.

The door gave to his anxious fingers. He could hear,

by his shoulder, quiet regular breathing. The man was asleep there in his bunk, his head toward Henry. Fear ran cold down Henry's naked spine. If the man flung an arm he could touch him. Yet he had to get out.

He crept along on hands and feet, feeling his way. He moved over a pair of pants, went carefully past a pail, crawled to the short ladder, where he could look up into a gently moving square of stars. His right hand, as he crouched, touched and recognized the stove and then came on something soft in crackling paper. One end was open, from which with delighted fingers he pulled out some sliced bread. It gave him courage to slide up the ladder as fast as he could, a small crouching shape.

Out there beyond the awning, in a gentle salt wind, the lighted night was enormous, a great moving expanse of black and silver water, with dark shapes of islands, near and far, and overhead the crowding festoons of stars. Eased, he ate new bread in handfuls, and drank a cup of water from the big glass demijohn. He sat outside the cockpit hidden from sight from the door, leaned his back against the cabin, and dangled his feet over the rippling water as the anchored boat gave and swung. Fear still lay undigested in him but he breathed deep and stared about with wonder and awe. In his entire life, he had never seen anything like this enormous wideness under the uplifted sky.

He stared over at an edge of moon rising orange out of a line of black. The flat-bottomed dinghy, on its short line, slapped on a dark moving tide. It was so still he heard the wind rippling the water. A night bird, a dark shape flying against the starts, let fall a single startling *quawk.*

He would not have known from here that that man was aboard. But suppose he woke suddenly and came on deck? The roots of Henry's hair prickled. What could he do then? Perhaps it would be better if he could let himself down into the soft dark water and swim over to that nearest island until the man and his boat went away. But he shuddered, staring at the water. It looked very deep. He had never been able to swim more than two or three strokes without panic. How did he know what things swam in it now, or what other things waited for him within the island's blackness?

He wished he had more bread and another cup of water. But now he did not dare to move across that open door. Perhaps the man was lying awake down there, watching the starry space. If he could get into the dinghy and drift away—the man would hear him. The boat could overtake him at once. For stealing the dinghy the man could have him locked up in jail.

The moon was higher and more white. Darkness grew among the mounds of islands. But in the east the sky was lifting and changing. Paleness overtook the stars. The dark line must be land across wide shimmering veils of water. Things were stirring in the trees of the dark nearby island. There were squawkings and croakings, quick flappings overhead. The air smelled newly fresh and salty. He could see the dinghy more plainly. Soon, he realized, it would be bright day.

There was nothing he could think of but crawling back down there into the foulness of that locker and hiding again. He tried to listen by the open door without showing himself. The man was absolutely quiet.

Henry got down the ladder soundlessly, crouched in the dark, listened. He heard only the little creakings and slappings of the boat. He crept forward, feeling his way. His heart hammered. He was coming up by the man's bunk. The cabin window was lighter. The man was a long shadow. He could not tell how his face was turned. How he was at the man's head. The black hole of the locker was just ahead. He held himself back from a wild dive into it, lifted a foot—

He heard himself yelling as iron fingers caught his elbow, turned him, grabbed his shoulder, flung him backward. He tried to crawl away on the floor. Then he was caught again, shaken until his head jerked, pushed upward, a bundle of arms and legs on deck in the pale light. He was set on his feet by the hand that gripped his aching arm. The man's face hung savagely over him.

"Stop that," he said. "Stop it. What do you think you're doing?"

Henry jerked himself loose. He could not breathe. He could not speak. He got his back against the cabin. The dark face was narrow and hateful, and the eyes were mean.

"You—you killed my alligator!" Henry cried.

"Killed your . . ." The whites of the man's eyes showed yellow. Lank hair blew on his head. He was tall and thin, with a big bump of Adam's apple in his long thin neck, but his bare arms and chest were ropy with muscle. "You crazy? Was it you busted my lock?"

Henry's head spun, his body was sore, his stomach was sick. Yet suddenly fear and desperation burned up in rage. "Yes, I busted it. I wanted to know. I found his skin—it's mine."

The man's lip curled over a broken tooth. "Like fun it's yours. You know what alligator skins get in Tampa now? Three dollar and seventy-fi' cents a foot. That one's two foot and a half."

Henry kept on shouting, "He was mine—you got no right—"

"Shut up that yelling," the man said. "That gang of hoodlums put you on board?"

"They did not. I was on board already. They busted up my cave and stole my things. I was hiding."

"You got no right to break my lock." Henry glared back at him, panting.

The man said, "You think I'm gonna take you home, you're crazy."

Henry said nothing. The man thought again. "Your folks'll be sending out the cops."

Henry shook his head. "They don't care."

The man went toward the cabin ladder. "I'm goin' to

turn you over to the park ranger at Rock Harbor," he said. "You're lucky he's not a cop."

Henry thought about that. Then he said clearly, "I'll tell him you killed my alligator! He'll see the hide—" He put his head down on the boards and fainted.

It was only a moment of nothingness. He woke with cold water on his face. From the stove down there was coming the reviving smell of bacon frying, the sound of eggs chuckling and popping in the pan.

The man yelled, "What you do with the bread?"

Henry said, "I ate it." The worst had happened. Now he knew only hunger.

Presently the man's long arm slid out on the deck toward him an enamel plate rich with food and a cup of coffee yellow with condensed milk. The man brought his cup of black coffee out on deck and sat on the stern seat, letting smoke from his cigarette blow white out of his nostrils. He said presently, "Get me some more coffee. Finish the eggs."

Henry moved carefully with the full cup. Then he sat on the deck with his feet on the ladder and scraped his plate. He sighed. "This is a keen boat," he said. "You live on it all the time?"

The man said, "What's your name?"

"Henry," he said. "What's yours?" He was amazed at how easy he felt. His hunger was gone. His head was clear. He began to feel fine.

The man said, "Arlie Dillon. You take that bucket

and get up some water and wash the dishes. Time to get goin'."

Henry lifted the bucket. Behind it, where he must have dropped it, was his knife. With that in the pocket of his ragged shorts, even if he had no shirt or sneakers, he was newly clothed. He lifted up the full bucket on its rope and went to scrubbing the eggy plates in saltwater. The whole world sparkled, the blue water, the dark green leaves on the little island under the brilliant sunny sky.

Dillon was forward at the bow hauling on his anchor. When it came up and he came back to start his engine, Henry said, "Where's Rock Harbor?"

The man tossed his chin toward the line of land to the east. His brown fingers twiddled precisely the complicated metal of the engine. Henry took the plates below. The cabin was a mess of tossed stuff. The locker door forward was swinging. He went to shut it, making sure that the alligator skin was there where he could put his hand on it. He walked back, noticing sharply where the gun was, the fishing rods, the food. There were expensive looking reels and well-sharpened knives on a knife board. There were a few frowsy comic books in a rack, some charts, lanterns, flashlights. There was everything anybody could need and a lot of things he couldn't guess the use of.

The engine started its roaring racket as he hopped up on deck. Suddenly the boat was off, in a spray of dazzling white. Dillon sat on the coaming, steering with a careless foot on the long tiller. Henry stood clinging to the cabin roof, staring forward in the salt wind, grinning in unspeakable delight. It was racing, it was flying. Blue water and foam streaked by. The spray fanned out from the bow in snow and a million trillion flashing diamonds. The speed lifted the big bow so that it leaped over the little waves, banged hard down on them, leaped and banged and raced, as if it beat down the watery miles underfoot. When Dillon changed her course to westward, the boat swerved and curved like a great bird in flight.

The whupping bumps jarred up along Henry's skinny body from his naked heels to his hipbones, to his bare ribs and the loosened jaw in his head. His knees gave to it as his feet and hands clung. His whole body was battered and warmed and delighted by it. His eyes blinked in the hard pour of wind and the stings of spray as the hair on his skull seemed plucked up by the roots. The morning sea was brilliant, pale green glass, streaked and shadowed with more kinds of green than he could think of the names for, jewels he had never heard of streaking beyond the shining snow of spray.

In his whole life, he had never known anything so wonderful.

He turned to yell happily at the man crouched over the tiller. His narrowed eyes under the straw brim were dark and fixed on something far ahead. His naked chest was yellowed, his figure in the stained pants dark against all the flash and brilliance and boil of the wake spinning behind, under the high dome of blue light. In the midst of Henry's new exaltation, his relief and surprise at the food and the lack of threats, he felt a stab of the same emotion he had known when he had first laid eyes on this man, a chill of hatred and distrust.

As he looked away, he could see at least that the boat was not heading in the direction of the place Dillon had said was Rock Harbor.

They moved at that speed, in all that thunder, for two or three hours.

Sometimes they saw single boats in the green, clear distance, with single fishermen in them huddled motionless over their lines. Once from a nearby boat a man lifted an arm and Dillon stared at him slowly and grudgingly flicked a finger. The land far away to the east was set with the tiny shapes of houses. The wide space of sunny green water around them was marked by low mounds of islands such as he had first seen in moonlight, dark green islands on which the trees came down to the water's edge and showed only brown shadows below dipping leaves. Birds rose over them and flapped and fished in shallows between them—white birds that he thought were gulls and great gray-brown pelicans hurling themselves, beak down like dive bombers, at some fish below. Two great dark birds with forked tails and huge arched spreading wings seemed to float in the air over the treetops with no motion at all. He could not ask what they were because Dillon could hardly have heard his shout over the engine's racket. He clung and felt himself grinning.

There was a larger island just ahead, the dark oily green leaves an impenetrable wall about it. Henry looked to see the boat swerve about it. It held its course straight.

Dillon leaned forward and snapped off his ignition. The boat rushed forward in the stillness. The dinghy came up fast and was stopped. The boat lay still, rocking a little in its own wash.

"No sense getting anywhere too soon," Dillon said. He stood up and stretched.

Henry said, "Where are we going?"

His eyes glinted at Henry before he turned to haul at the dinghy's painter. "Get a mess of fish," he said.

"Why didn't you fish out there, where those men were fishing?" Henry said.

Dillon glanced at him contemptuously.

"Commercial fishermen," he said.

"What do they catch? Do they get lots?"

"Depends on what's runnin'. Sea trout, yellowtail, amberjack. Used to be so full of fish round here you'd run your boat over schools of 'em. Crawfish and shrimp in the rocks. Reef fish, all kinds. Catch all you want. Fill up your boat."

"What happened?"

"Too many people," Dillon said and spat into the water.

Henry stared ahead to the trees. "What you think you can get in here?"

"You wanta come along? Then don't talk so much."

41

It seemed to Henry that Dillon was paddling the boat, standing up and dipping an oar leisurely, this side or that as he chose, straight into a thick wall of trees. The bow pushed into cool shadows. The shadowy water was clear brown, flecked and netted with gold below over muddy shallows. Then he saw the trees open out into a narrow waterway, into which the boat passed. Leaves brushed alongside.

The trees grew out of gray, arched, branching roots that stood in the brown water. The island seemed to be no more than groups of trees on either side of a channel in which the boat moved quietly.

"Mangrove," Dillon said as if Henry had asked him. "They're all over."

A slender bird trailing long legs flipped away before them from higher up among the branches. "Little green heron. Lots of 'em got nests up there. See?" There were untidy piles of sticks in the crotches of innumerable branches where birds were lifting and flying away from them with crying, complaining voices. In the nearest nest Henry could see two small fuzzy heads bobbing. There were baby birds in all of the nests, hundreds of them. The mother birds flew in creaking unhappy circles high over the trees, against the sun. To see them all there gave Henry such a shiver of excitement that he nearly choked. But all he could think to whisper was, "Are they good to eat?"

Dillon said, "Naw."

There were rusty black birds making grating sounds

ahead. "Grackles," Dillon said. Little brown birds hopped and jerked along branches. Overhead in a bare space of brightness he caught glimpses of white birds sailing free on free white wings. The sudden rustle and beat of all the birds roused a new and deep delight in him. He could not get enough of watching them. He had had dreams of flying, but not like that. It was a kind of exaltation.

They were coming out into a shallow bay among the trees, quite hidden. The water deepened under them, running in shadow beneath the great tangled roots of the trees. Staring down where old roots went down fuzzy with water weeds into the mud, Henry saw hundreds of tiny fish all swinging together one way or another, their tiny dots of eyes all alike, their tiny bodies like sticks of gray glass. Suddenly they all flipped away. He saw little crabs crawling down there in the clear salt. Then a few larger fish seemed to hang there, clear gray, as if the light shone through them, with fine black lines at their eyes. Then they were gone. Then three bigger ones came nose to nose together, their tails moving them as gently as the water.

He had been sitting so still and watching so intently he had not been aware that the man had been making a few quiet motions behind him. He was startled when a short fish line sang by his ear and its baited hook and sinker plopped no more heavily than a broken twig into the open water ahead. The bait was trailed near the roots but clear of them.

The biggest fish of the lot curved toward the bait. Its

gray nose touched it, went past. Then it was back, hovering. It snapped. There was a jerk and a white froth of water. The fish fled. The line jiggled after, the reel clicked. The fish shook the hook like a little dog. The reel clicked again. The fish was coming in.

A net handle was poked at Henry. His hands shook a little but he got the hoop deep in the water. The fish hung over it. He lifted—there the fish hung, flapping and spattering. Soon it was in the boat and Dillon put his foot on it and got out the hook.

"Mangrove snapper," Dillon said. "There's another. Shrimp in the pail. Bait the other line."

Henry lost his bait. His hook caught in the leaves. His cast was no good. He nearly caught himself in the eye. Dillon caught two more snapper. Then there were no more. Everything was quiet down there. The little fish were back. A crab walked on the mud. It was hot. Henry was not even watching his line. Then Dillon hissed at him. The biggest snapper in the world darted straight for Henry's bait, took it, ran with it. Henry waved his rod but could not find the handle of his reel. He shouted. He stood up. He sat down. But the fish was still there on his hook. Somehow he brought it nearer. Dillon netted it. It thumped on the floor boards.

"I caught it," Henry said staring. "I've fished and fished but I never caught a fish in my whole life before."

"I do' knows I ever saw a bigger snapper," Dillon said. "Get us a couple more now and we'll eat good."

Dillon fried the pieces of white fish meat he had

cleaned while Henry hung in the open doorway over the galley, inhaling the fragrance. He would remember later the three gray and white seagulls that had flashed down to pick up the fish cleanings with thin black beaks, their round black eyes fixed, their pink feet dangling as they swept past and blew up over the boat. His fingers had longed to be able to reach up and touch those firm, feathery, white breasts. But now he was all one ache of hunger.

It seemed to him then, watching Dillon's fingers expert with knife and pan, that there was nothing Dillon could not do well. It was queer to admire a man and hate him at the same time.

When he had eaten his first plateful, which was passed to him amazingly heaped with buttery hot grits, he knew he had never tasted food like this in his life. He ate two helpings and Dillon said to finish up everything left in the pan before he cleaned things up. Henry burst out, "I bet you're the best fisherman and the best fish fryer in the whole bright and shining world." He couldn't help it. He felt too good.

Dillon only grunted, but there was a pleased crease around his mouth. He went and lay down and slept, his face tight and secret. Henry slipped glances at him, trying not to make too much noise. Then he curled up on the deck and slept also.

He woke, aching only a little. Dillon was staring out to the west where the sun was still high. "Come on," he said, pulling in the dinghy. "You ever see a crocodile nest?"

The roaring engine carried them flying out from among the trees, west to the low mainland shore. It looked lower and browner and more desolate than the tree-covered islands but birds were flying over it. Sometimes Dillon named them, and he stared after them as if learning the names was to take a kind of possession of their airy freedom. "Cormorant," he murmured over and over as one after another of the glossy black birds with their long necks outstretched slipped off stakes or channel markers where they had been solemnly looking for fish, and skimmed with quick black wing beats the surface of the water. Now in the afternoon light the green glassy look was gone, and everything—sky and bay—was a soft watery blue.

"Madeira Bay, this is," Dillon said. "There's the beach ahead."

"Are there people there?"

"Nobody. Nothin' but birds and raccoons and 'possum. Maybe a panther now and then. Deer back in. But crocodiles. They make their nests here."

"You mean, alligators."

"Crocs, I said. Don't you know the difference? Crocs got a long narrow snout with teeth coming through the upper jaw. Clay colored, ugly lookin'. They live in saltwater. No good for hides. People used to shoot 'em for the fun of it. They're pretty shy now. Haven't seen a croc in years."

He drew up the dinghy when the engine was silent, motioned Henry in, and paddled standing up. When

46

the bow grated they had to get out in a foot of shallow water in which Henry was startled to find himself sinking almost to the knee in white oozy clay. "Keep goin'. You'll be all right," Dillon said. But he got out on the rough sand beach with relief. It ran empty between the clear water of the bay and yellow-gray matted scrub trees, with a few coco-palms. Long-legged little sandpipers trotted up the beach away from them.

"Look. Here's where she went," Dillon said. There was a broad trail through the sand, blurred and old. The ground under the scrubby bushes was soft and mucky. Dillon turned here and there, following the trail. "Here," he said. "Here's where she laid her eggs." There was a two foot mound of coarse hot sand in an opening. Dillon scraped the sand away.

"Under all that sand," Henry said.

"Yep. I figure the croc lays 'em deep and kicks the sand over with her hindlegs and her tail. Has to, to keep the raccoons from digging them out. Look. Here's a couple of old eggs that didn't hatch." He uncovered some round things like gray stones. Henry touched one. It was like leather.

"Is there a little one in that one now?" he asked.

"Naw. These didn't hatch. She musta laid a whole lot. Then I figure she musta come back here to help them out when they're hatching. Alligator, now, she makes a nest inland, on a bank by freshwater and heaps up a lot of old grass and weeds over them that rot in the hot sun and hatch the eggs. Time comes, the 'gator wants out, it's got a little hook on the end of its nose, like an egg tooth, and it cracks the shell and comes out and heads for the water. You can hear them squeaking in the shell. The old 'gator don't have to pay them any heed. They're so lively they take care of themselves.

"But the crocodiles, now. I figure she buries 'em so deep in the hot sand to hatch that she has to come back and help claw all this sand off them when she hears them squeaking. Maybe she drives off the 'coons. Maybe not so many hatch. I do' know.

"Look there, where she went to her own hole." They followed the trail through higher bushes, smelling sweet in the sun. "There's where she's been holed up, in there."

"Do you see her?" Henry said with excitement and a certain fear.

"Can't tell if she's there or not and I'm not the one to poke her up." They bent and stared at a shadowy mound under low branches. There was a hole nearby. "Here's where she comes out. She stays deep in there, daytimes. I knew a man once was huntin' crocs and he stepped on a croc's mound and went right through with one leg, right onto the croc. He could feel it moving. Like to yelled his head off."

"Did—did it bite him?"

"Couldn't open its jaws that much, I guess, though a croc's jaws are both hinged. But when the man got loose the croc came chasin' after him, so he shot it. Prob'ly wouldn't hurt him none. The alligator's the savage one."

A bird with black wings and red legs came over fast,

shrieking. It circled high and low near them, landed in an open place and seemed to crumple up. "It's hurt," Henry said. "The wing's broken."

"Just a stilt. There's lots of stilts in there. They build their nests around a little pond. This one thinks we're going to steal her eggs and she's tryin' to lead us away from them. Noisy birds."

Henry looked back from the beach. Half a dozen stilts were flying round and round back there, fast, their red legs dangling, keeping up that regular shrieking cackle.

Wading back to the boat Henry heaved a great sigh of satisfaction at a world so empty and so crammed with wonders. "Now we'll get goin'," Dillon said.

Madeira Bay

IT was the middle of the afternoon. The water was a
darker blue, with wind under white clouds in a bluer
sky. The boat moved on its same dazzling, roaring flight,
but on the roughened waves the spray came high over
like bucketfuls of white shot. The bumps were harder
and the foamy water streaked past faster and faster.

"Where are we going?" Henry shouted, turning his
delighted, salty, dripping face toward the man crouched
over the tiller. Dillon nodded toward the southwest.

More islands went by. The mainland went on in a con-
tinuous changing line, nearer or farther. Only the rushing
water was always there, the roaring engine, the speeding
boat. Henry clung and wished that it would never end.

Two hours or so more and Dillon turned off the ignition. The boat slid forward in silence and little by little,
its dinghy following awkwardly, came to rest. There was
an island between them and the mainland. They drifted
toward the lengthening shadow of its trees. Dillon flung
out his light anchor. He stood for a while looking ahead
and far away, where two or three white boats were moving as if drawn by the same thread. He moved back, quick
and light as a cat, by the coaming along by the cabin
and swung down into the cockpit without a sound.

Henry watched his dark closed face with caution
and said nothing. Dillon swung down to the icebox and
came up with a can of beer, which he sat drinking, his
feet up on the stern seat. His hat was pushed back from
his bleached and wet-looking forehead. His narrowed
gaze was fixed far away.

Henry got up softly after a while. He was amazed
that he was so hungry again. Dillon said, "Get me another beer."

Henry watched him with the old apprehension. When
people sat and drank—beer or liquor, whatever it was—
one drink after another, with that queer fixing of attention on something far away that was really inside their
own heads, anything could happen. But Dillon only
said, "There's some pop down there. Make yourself a
sandwich." It was peanut butter and the pop was orange,
icy and sweet. He sat on the deck with his legs out, ate,
and was reassured. About the boat the water chuckled.

Over there in the distance where the white slivers of

boats moved under the yellowing sky, something glittered. "What's that?" Henry said.

"Flamingo. Get me another beer." After he drank again his mouth was more bitter. "I lived there," he said.

Henry glanced back at him. "Where do you live now?"

Dillon drank his beer, tossed the can overboard. He looked heavily at Henry and rapped with his knuckles on the plank next to him. "Here." After a while he said, "They kicked us out."

"Who?"

"The park. Everglades Park. That's what's there now. All that's left of Flamingo. Some fancy buildings. They tore down our houses."

Henry said, "How could they? Didn't they pay you?"

"Sure they paid us." Dillon swept his hand at the boat. "You think this makes up for it?" He took a long breath as if his words were pulled out, one by one. "What it used to be like was—we had everything. Nobody to interfere. Nobody to say, 'You can't do this—you can't do that.' Look,"—he pointed with his long brown finger and it was only then that Henry thought he'd had too much beer—"look, there was these little houses on pilings. You'd see 'em stand in a kind of shimmer. When the tide came up, maybe a hurricun—why, the water'd go under 'em. Make no diff'rence. Boats out there in the water. Some little wharves. Boats comin' and goin'. Cows back there. Come moskeeter season, my daddy drove the cows up to Homestead. 'Skeeters drive the cows crazy. We'd go out in the boats—make no diff'rence to us. We was tough. When they was birds—curlews, all like that, we'd go get us all the curlews we wanted.

"Come up to one of these rookeries in the dark. All this white curlews on the nests. Turn on the lights. Take clubs to 'em. In one night we'd get seventy-hundred dollars' worth of plumes. Used to be, my daddy'd sell 'em in Tampa, Key West, Miamer—plenty money. Then these men come snoopin'—these Aud'bon fellers. They past a law you couldn't sell no more plumes and nobody could buy 'em. What'd we care? Load up the boat, sell 'em in Havana. Big money. Time they got to payin' good money in Tampa for alligator hides—why, they's plenty alligator hides. Last time I remember my daddy, me, and some more found us a lake full of 'gators—way up east of Little Shark River. Thick as sticks. We cleaned um out, ever'one.

"There was a long time there when one of my uncles raised a patch of corn and set him up a still—open shed right by the road. Nobody to stop him. The first road was just put in then but it was so rough not even pro'bitioners came down it. Made white mule, good as any west coast aggerdent. Sold it cheap to any boat put in here.

"That's the way it was then. Do what you want. That's the way it oughta be. I mind me the time some of these big bugs from Washington was down talkin' about makin' this a park—twenty years ago, it was. They was up Tarpon Bend in a houseboat havin' 'emselves a time. They went up the Little Shark in flat boats. Man told me that rowed 'em. Sun goin' down. Moon comin' up. All these long whites goin' over and plume birds rustlin' their wings. Them big bugs they stood up in the boats an' lost their breaths over all them birds goin' over, ohin' an' ahin'.

"Came night, they was back in the houseboat. Big one—all lit up so's you could see it in the black night over the black water. We was over on the next hammock camped, me and my daddy an' some from Everglades. The plumes on them plume birds was in prime condition.

"Some fool rowed up to that houseboat an' tole them big bugs we was lyin' there waitin' for them to get out before we went an' shot up that rookery. So what happen but some of them come over in a boat to where we was sittin' round our fire on this mound. They wouldn' say nothin' about us shootin' up the rookery. No sir. They was too polite for that. They just talked. Lettin' us know they was there, all big bugs—Washin'ton, New York, whereall—that'd scare us, they musta figured. Talked about the laws against plume huntin'.

"Next night, they's gone. Wasn't hardly a livin' bird we missed. Shine the light on them an' you could walk up and knock them down with clubs. Made five, six hundred dollars in Havana. I'll never forget it."

Henry was staring at him, trying to take it in. He didn't get all of it, except somebody was killing birds the way Dillon killed his alligator. Whose alligator, he'd said. Anybody's was his, that's the way he had it figured. Anybody's was his—like those big boys. Taking what they wanted, smashing the rest. Henry's spine was prickling with anger. He knew what it was to be hunted. He hated them all, those big boys and this narrow-faced man. They were all the same kind.

"So anyway, they decided to make this park of it and they did. They took ever'thing away from us—our houses, the plume birds, the alligators. Why, you couldn't even shoot you a deer."

Dillon's voice was slowing down as if the beer was dying in him. "We hadda get outa there where we'd all lived. Sure, they paid us for the houses and the land. Some men I know bought places down the Keys, took to fish-guidin' for tourists. Some of them got house-boats you could anchor here for the sea trout or up the west coast when the big schools of pampano or snook are running. My daddy died an' I got me this boat, best anybody could want. I made up my mind nobody's goin' to stop me takin' what I want." He was silent a long time. "No money in plumes anymore. But alligators now—if you can find where to look for them. . . ."

The afternoon was late. Birds were streaming over toward the land from the flats beyond which the sea to the south was shimmering lavender. Dillon glanced around him. His mouth was tight again as if he had not spoken a word. He hauled up his anchor, started his engine. They roared along a well-marked channel past mangrove clumps like bouquets of deep green leaves, in a green light from the orange-colored west. A whirl of white gulls was sliding down and blowing up by docks and boats.

A long building on pillars, more than half glass, took shape across the bay on the low shore. Palm trees were green beyond where cars moved and glittered.

In a little bay, Dillon cut his engine, tossed out his anchor. The sound of voices, a man's laugh, noises of cars came to them over the sheltered water. The smallest sailboat Henry had ever seen, the size of a well-painted packing box, slid past them with a little rippling under a bright blue sail no bigger than a tablecloth. Henry stared and laughed out loud. To his surprise, it was a small girl crouching at the tiller, just the size for the boat—a girl in a white shirt and shorts. Her pale yellow hair stuck out in a ponytail. She turned and stared at him. Her eyes were cool blue.

The first pink and orange of a sunset flared high over the flat land to the west. Dillon stood up and stretched. His voice came harshly to Henry's ears as he sat musing without thought, his eyes stretched with the wideness of the world.

"There's a man here that goes up to Homestead ever'day or so," Dillon said. "I'll give him your ticket money. He'll put you on the bus to go home. Your ma'll be callin' out the cops."

Henry's eyes stared up at him out of a face suddenly pinched. The old fear drew hard at his heart. He said huskily, "She don't care." Dillon did not hear him, busy with the boat.

Henry looked around him slowly, fighting despair.

Maybe it was true. Maybe he had to go back to that crowded back room and those streets, from this world he could not have imagined existed, wide and quiet, windy, free. Men here were untrustworthy too, he thought suddenly, looking away from Dillon. But there was room here. He had no words for what, suddenly, the wide water and the sky, the fish—above all, the birds—had begun to mean to him. But he knew that if he had to leave it now, something in him that had started to grow would never live.

His thoughts ran here and there, confused and desperate, like trapped ants. When Dillon drew up the dinghy, got in, jerked his head at him, Henry sat in the stern, gripping his hands between his knees. Dillon rowed. Henry no longer saw the color of the sky. He looked down at his torn and filthy shorts, at his dirty lumps of knees, his bony legs, his bare, burned feet. His naked back shivered a little with the cooler wind and with defeat.

What could he do? He knew again how helpless he was, how small and insignificant. He hardly remembered his own name anymore. He was just something that this man, rowing effortlessly, could order about with all the ruthless and terrible authority of adults.

The dinghy moved past the docks where boats lay close—fine fishing boats with outriggers for fish lines, boats gleaming with metal and white paint, a long yacht with a wheelhouse and fancy chairs under the after awning. The little sailboat was tied up to a float next to it, from which a man in dungarees walked up the plank, saw Dillon, and raised a slow hand to him.

Dillon took one hand from an oar and jerked a thumb in the direction where he was heading.

The man said, "See you."

Twilight dimmed. Strings of lights shone out over the docks, tall lights in rows among the trees of the parking places. Beyond the building on its high pillars was a long frame of brilliant electricity.

The dinghy slid along a weedy, bulkheaded bank, to which Dillon, already shadowy, made his easy cat leap. He snagged the painter around a post. "Hurry up," he said and began walking toward a lower cluster of lights and cars.

Henry got out slowly. He had to. He saw that. But something hard and sure was growing up in him like the rage that had first possessed him, that had brought him to this. Trotting silently not to lose sight of Dillon, there was nothing in his mind but an increasing purpose and words that repeated themselves over and over. His lips whispered them, taking slow, deep breaths through stiffened nostrils. The words said, "I won't go."

Flamingo

HE sat before a little table in a crowded, brightly lighted trailer, eating a stupendous meal. He ate brown pot roast and gravy on a big baked potato, with carrots in it and bits of soft cooked onion, even peas. He had a big slice of bread thick with butter and a big glass of milk that left cream all around his mouth. He wanted to eat slowly because everything tasted so good but his hunger, that old constant companion, kept him eating as fast as he could swallow. And while he was doing that, with more in a big dish right in front of him, with a serving spoon pointed directly at his hand, the big brown woman who lived here went on cooking. This long trailer seemed to Henry, with all its shining equipment, to be truly magnificent. From its wall oven, she was taking out an apple pie so hot, so brown crusted, so fragrant of sugar and cinnamon, that his eyes widened and his mouth watered all over again.

They were alone in the trailer together. Her name was Mrs. Pearl. She had black eyes and gray hair, two gold teeth, a big mouth, and dimples that showed as often as he took another mouthful. To add to all that, he had been ordered to scrub in the nearby shower house with soap that smelled of lemons. His clean hair stuck up over his head in drying wisps. And he had on a clean mended blue shirt, only a little too long for him in the turned-up sleeves, clean faded denim shorts, and a pair of sneakers, only the least little bit worn, that fitted him perfectly.

When he had knocked again at her door with his wide smile breaking out all over his face, she had said, "Well, you certainly look a lot less like something the cat brought in."

Arlie Dillon had brought him here, left him outside while he knocked and went in and talked—mumble, mumble. Henry could not make out a word, although he strained his ears. The woman's slow voice said, "Well, I never," and "What about that?" and then, "But where is he? Bring him in."

He guessed that he must have looked as lost and dirty and miserable as he knew he felt, because she took one look at him and began to order him around. He did not notice what became of Dillon. By the time he had finished a big piece of pie, over which she had poured half a little pitcherful of cream so thick it went "glop," he knew all about her. She was a chambermaid over in the big fancy motel beyond the main park building. Her husband worked at the lunch counter. Their son, a year younger than he was and much bigger, lived with her sister in Homestead during the week so that he could go to school. He came down to the park on weekends and helped around the docks.

Just about everybody who worked about headquarters lived in these big trailers in their own trailer place by the water's edge. A lot of people who came here to work didn't stay long, she told him, because it was too far away from towns and there were no schools. But Mrs. Pearl and her husband liked it fine and Jimmy loved it. Besides, Mrs. Pearl had been brought up over in the Ten Thousand Islands. "When Pappy taken the boys out fishin' or plumin', they wasn't another human for miles around 'ceptin' Mama and we girls. Mama was always scared to death some of those alligators that was always layin' right there in the river bellerin' would walk up on their bow legs an eat up the baby. Mama come from real nice people in Tampa and she like to never let us forget it."

In almost the same breath she said, "An' how about your poor mama frettin' an' worryin' up there thinkin' you're lost or I don't know what? I bet you'll be mighty tickled to get back to her."

He pushed his plate away. With the cleanness and

the good food his purpose rose up in him, calm and shining. He looked at her carefully, trying to decide how much he dared to tell her.

"This man Arlie Dillon's gone to see doesn't go up to Homestead until the day after tomorrow, but I tole him you're welcome as the flowers in May to sleep in Jimmy's bed an' eat with me here. There's a ranger goin' up tomorrow could take you but Arlie didn't seem to think he'd want me to ask him."

Henry tightened his pleased grin. Good. Then his threat to tell the Rock Harbor ranger about that alligator skin aboard had worked. It had been only a desperate guess. Dillon was nervous about rangers, and that was for sure. It gave Henry his first small sense of power. He could put his hand on that skin in a minute. His mind made itself up firmly not to leave it there, either. It was his more than it was Dillon's. He didn't know what he could do with it. Maybe it would be too risky to show it to a ranger. But he could bargain with it.

Mrs. Pearl was going right on talking, her dimples and her gold teeth winking as she cleared up the dishes and washed them in a neat little sink that came out of a wall, with bright faucets gushing hot and cold water. He was lost in smiling admiration of all the elegant varnished neatness of the trailer, all electric lights and cupboards with chrome handles and little glass shelves filled with funny china animals and little green plants in pots and even a small TV. He was wondering what would happen to all that clutter of little things if they hitched up the trailer to a car and ran it over a bumpy road, when he was startled to realize what she was saying. "I tole Arlie Dillon I'd take you right away to telephone your poor distracted mama, so's she'd know you'd be home day after tomorrow on the Homestead bus and could stop worrying. If it was me I'd be outa my mine."

He almost blurted it out then, that he'd made up his mind not to go home at all. But he knew too well how little he could trust any adult. He almost said, "She prob'ly hasn't noticed." Somehow he couldn't say that either, in the face of her cushiony motherliness. He only managed to mumble, "She hasn't got a phone."

She spoke thoughtfully, "I never hold with talking to the police. But there must be somebody, some neighbor. Everybody must know around there that they've missed you."

He looked at her.

She just didn't know what it was like to live in one of those crowded apartment places—the quarrelling, the screaming, the children crying. No one knew how many children there were or whose they were. Nobody like her, he thought patiently, in this place where there were miles and miles and miles with no people at all, only birds and fish, could know what people were like when they lived jammed in together. Too many people. He saw it, suddenly. Maybe his mother couldn't help the way she was. Maybe she couldn't stand it any better than he could. It was a sobering, an aging, thought. He said, "There's a man on the next floor maybe I could get him to talk to her."

"Why, of course, honey," she said. "He'd be glad to, I'm sure. They'll all be so glad to know you're all right. Now I'm just goin' to put on a clean dress and we'll go up to the pay telephone—and look, I'll tell you what, there's a movie up to the main building tonight we can go to."

It was full dark when he scrambled into her big car, almost as big as the trailer, he thought, and they swung up the dark way from the trailer park to the main road. The wind came soft. Lights of the park building were bright between them and the darkened sea. Dillon was off somewhere, perhaps muttering to that dockman. What they talked about, he was sure, was something the rangers would not hear.

"Isn't it pretty?" Mrs. Pearl shouted. "When I's a girl, if I'd ever have thought it would be like this, I declare! We'd come around the cape in our sailboat to the fish house wharf. They was only a few unpainted board shacks up on stilts because of hurricane water, but Mama liked to set and rock on Aunt Mary Dillon's porch. It had screens, even if they was rusty. There was nothin' but cistern water to drink and Mama always said there musta been dead rats in it. She took her tea boilin', waitin' for Papa to get himself a skinful at the still back by the road. Half the time, he never sobered up till he sailed the boat

clear home. An' mosquitoes—my lan! You couldn't
hardly open up your mouth to breathe.

"Ol' man Roberts used to say when he was diggin'
holes for his garden, when he wanted fertilizer, all he
did was reach out and get him a handful of mosquitoes
for ever' hole. Seems to me the ones we had up the west
coast was kinda slower. I guess we'll go to the pay telephone by the motel office. I wished you could see those
rooms—half plate glass and pink tiles in the bathrooms."

He dragged one leg after the other out of the car.
Mrs. Pearl put the quarters and dimes in his fists and
hovered outside the red phone booth, nodding encour-
agement through the glass.

He had a time looking up the name in the book. The
last name was O'Neill, but he was not sure of the first
name, so he had to go down the page to the right address. Then he read everything it said over the telephone
about how to get long distance. Then he forgot the number and had to look it up all over again. By that time she
had seen somebody she knew in the lighted motel office
and had walked over to talk to her. He stood nervously
on tiptoe to put the coins in, clang, clank. Then he gave
the operator the number in such a feeble voice she asked
him to repeat it until he was shouting. There was a long
wait, in which Mrs. Pearl looked over at him through
two windows and waved and smiled. He was just beginning to think he was stupid not to have kept the money
and just made believe he was telephoning when Mr.

O'Neill's heavy voice sounded in his ear. The operator told him, "Homestead is calling."

Henry said, "Mr. O'Neill this is Henry Bunks you know my mother upstairs in Number Ten, Mrs. Helen Williams—why, will you please go up and tell her please I—"

Mr. O'Neill said, "Who?"

Henry shouted it all over again. It said above the phone that he had only three minutes. "Tell her I got a job on a boat, with a man, I'm fine, I'm not coming home for a while, you tell her Mr. O'Neill, thanks a lot, I'm all right, I'm fine—g'bye."

Mr. O'Neill was shouting, "Who'd you say? Where are you?" Henry hung up, firmly and carefully, and banged open the door. Mrs. Pearl reached her hands out for him and asked, "Wasn't she glad? Did she cry? Did you tell her when you'll get home? Will she come and meet you?"

It was too hard to explain. He just nodded and smiled and pretty soon she stopped talking to the other woman and they got into the big car and curved around into the lights of the main building. Henry was so excited he felt his face grinning and grinning.

He remembered that evening upstairs in the big bright lobby: Mrs. Pearl's husband, Jack, and the double ice-cream cone he was given over the shining counter, and the movie about little animals in a desert, and the lights going up again over all the people who were there— men and women from the motels in fancy sports clothes and people like the Pearls who worked here and a ranger or two in their neat gray-green uniforms and people from the boats.

The small girl from the sailboat was there in a clean pink dress. He remembered her father, the big man in white pants and shirt. She asked, "Are you staying on your boat? Where's your father?" But he just shook his head at her.

Mrs. Pearl made his bed on the backseat of the trailer so soft he could hardly sleep on it, worrying what he could do to keep from being sent home. At least he had one whole day more.

Then it was morning, and Mrs. Pearl was frying pancakes and sausage and Mr. Pearl had already gone to work. If he hurried, she said, he could ride over to the main building with her and do anything he wanted, all day long. Mr. Pearl would give him his lunch at the lunch counter.

The world was so bright and new he could not help feeling gay. The bright sky was enormous over the flat lands—the queer flat lands colored yellow and straw-color, bright green with weeds and low bushes, and streaked blue with swamp water. All beyond to east and south was the expanse of sea as bright as sliver. Against it the islands were dark and boats shone white. The buildings along the shore stood out against it sharply, but far away the land and sea merged into a kind of haze of sun glitter. The wind was strong, warm and salty, and birds were tossing high in it.

When she let him out on the sidewalk he stood and

stared up with his mouth open at two great dark birds like arrows on rigid wings curved like long bows that seemed to hang in the stream of air like fish in clear water. One suddenly soared and turned slowly as if his wing tip were a pivot. The other rose, soaring as the tide of air carried him—so easy, so free.

She looked out to see what he stared at. "Man-o'-war birds," she said. "Ain't they the prettiest? Seems as if most anybody'd be perfectly happy just to be up there almost to the clouds, hangin' and soarin'. Sometimes they don't come down for hours. Then they only fish off the top of the water or steal fish some other birds caught. Their wings so long they can't hardly take off from a beach. They have to get the wind under 'em or a little bush, and then they go back again—high up—high as the clouds—if you only could . . ."

She had started the car and left him still staring upward at the great birds before he thought, How did a grown-up come to think like that? He walked up the ramp to the second story of the building raised on high pillars so that high tides or hurricane water could sweep under the upper floor. He stood a long time staring out to the bright sea in the long screened upper corridor, with tourists swirling around him. People made no difference to him, if they could not boss him. He walked wistfully behind a park ranger in the glory of his uniform, wondering what would happen if he said to him suddenly, "Mister, help me not to have to go home."

It would not do any good.

He looked over and saw Arlie Dillon's gray boat swimming idly at anchor. It didn't look as if anyone was on board. Then his eye was caught by the funny small blue sail. The boat was coming smoothly around the end of the last dock, heading into the wind. The girl in it was a small dab of white. Crazy kind of a little girl, he thought. He wandered through a door that said MUSEUM and stood in dimness, spellbound by the lighted exhibits along the wall—snakes, birds, turtles, alligators, crocodiles. He could see the difference, just as the sign and Dillon said. He pored over a map of the area. The boat had come down the Sounds from Miami in the night. He had caught fish near some of those Keys. There was the place they had found the crocodile nest—Madeira Bay. Here they were at Flamingo, the very place. It gave him a pleasant feeling to know just where he was. It was a long, long road back to Miami.

He pored over pictures of Indians, black bears, panthers, and raccoons. If he could only watch them. He spent a long time looking at the picture of the man some of those plume hunters had killed, Guy Bradley, the first Audubon Society Warden. He had lived just here at Flamingo. There was a picture of the funny small unpainted houses on stilts that were scattered over the flat wheel-marked land. Dillon had lived here, and the other men who used to kill the birds for their plumes.

There was a picture of one, A SNOWY EGRET, with a round dark eye and over its head a shining haze of feathers. He felt his angry hatred rising in him again.

Dillon liked to kill things like that. Some men just like him had killed Guy Bradley. It made him feel sad and old and heavy thinking of a world full of people like that. What could you do?

It was better to look at birds even if they were stuffed—all their swift electric aliveness dulled. But it was easier to study them like this, the brown pelican with its great pouch and webbed feet, the cormorants, the green heron that he knew. He told himself he would surely recognize a great white heron stalking by itself in some glittery solitude, also the American egret, and the blue and white heron. He longed to see a whole flight of the strange pink birds labeled ROSEATE SPOONBILL. There was a stilt, red legs and all. He grinned to remember its crazy squawking. But suppose they sent him home before he had seen any more?

The thought disturbed him so much that he hurried out. He had to find something to do, quick.

He was hungry too. He was pushing along to the lunch counter and Mr. Pearl, through the swing doors to the great upper room, when that same little girl in white shorts, with her ponytail tied with a white ribbon, stopped him.

There were freckles on her impudent small nose. Her eyes were bluer than ever. Or maybe they were a light green. But they were bright and fixed him.

"Hello, boy," she said. "Where are you going—what's your name—I've got a loaf of bread—come and feed the birds."

"I'm hungry," he said sullenly.

"All right. I want a chicken sandwich and a choc'late milkshake—my father pays for it—do you like seagulls— do you like herring gulls best or do you like laughing gulls—after we've had lunch and we've fed them you can come out sailing in my boat."

Gulf Water

S HE really was not like any girl he had ever known. Not that he paid any attention to girls, except to ignore them. Her name was Agatha and she was younger than he by at least six months, enough for contempt. Except that he was unable to be contemptuous of her. Her small brown hands were expert at the tiller of the funny flat-bottomed sailboat she called a "pram," and he admired the way she handled her blue sail. The glittering yacht, the largest boat at the dock, was where she lived.

They sailed there after they had thrown the bread, piece by piece, to a screaming wheeling mob of gulls. He picked up from her instantly the knowledge that brown ones just turning white were immature, and the fat white-and-gray ones were adult herring gulls, and the small, neat, black-headed ones were the laughing gulls. Over their heads the sound of birds among the rustling, swooping, lifting snow of wings was a faint high mewing—a half-crying queer laughter. They laughed out loud together, never getting tired of seeing a bird in fast flight snatch a tossed crust without a change of wing beat. It was even funnier when a wheeling bird, intent on a thrown bread scrap, crashed breast on into another or undercut it to the prize. Gulls came from everywhere, crowds of gulls circling, dropping to the water, flapping up again. Then the bread was gone.

They sailed around the inner bay, and somehow she got him started talking. He sat in the middle seat before the sail, looking dreamily over the water, doing what she told him to when she was ready to shift sail from one side to the other. She had asked him his name again and called the man in the boat his father. He had shaken his head absently and said, "My father died. Or maybe he went off. I don't know."

"You don't know?"

He said, "Well, my mother never told me. Anyway, she's got another husband."

"Your—your stepfather? Is he nice?"

"He's mostly drunk," he said absently. His eyes were on Dillon's boat, which they had just sailed past. It was empty. A cabin door was open. He thought of that skin in there. "And my mother, too. They get drunk a lot together."

Her exclamation drew his eyes to her face. She was staring at him in wide-eyed horror. "They get drunk?" she said faintly.

His face was suddenly hot and red. Any of the children he knew would understand that. The mother or the father drank. Maybe there wasn't any father. One boy's father was in jail. One boy lived with his grandmother because his mother had run off and left him. Something like that happened all the time where he lived. A lot of the kids had to take care of themselves. The gang of boys on their street was more important than any of their families could possibly be.

But looking at her he saw a different world where children were safe and well-cared-for and loved. There was always plenty of the best food there and good clothing and expensive toys like this boat she sailed as deftly as a boy. He thought she looked at him with disgust, as if he were some kind of a dirty bug.

He felt something he had never felt before. Not rage. Shame. But why did she have to look at him as if it were his own fault?

"I got away from all that, didn't I? Well, I'm not going back."

Her look changed. "Who wants you to?" she asked.

"Dillon. He says I gotta go back on the bus from Homestead tomorrow morning. But I don't have to. It's vacation."

Excitement made her voice husky. "Look. Let's go ask my father—"

"Don't you dare," he said. "He'll say I gotta go home. They're all alike. Besides, Dillon wants to get me outa here. He's afraid I'll report him." He told her about his alligator.

Her eyes, wide now with admiration and enthusiasm, exalted him. "You can't go," she said, shipping a wave absently. "Look, my father hates people to kill things. He'll think of something. Let's go talk to him now."

She came about deftly as he ducked the flapping sail. The small boat joggled and bounced toward the dock.

"There he is now," she said.

There had been such news of snook and jack running that morning that the dock was almost empty of fishing boats, fishermen, and tourists. Henry looked over, narrowing his gaze against the glare of the sun. "No," he said. "I don't want to. He's talking to Dillon now. If they're talking about me, turn around. I want to go away."

"Keep quiet," she whispered. "We can listen, can't we?" She ran the pram alongside the float and let down her sail that flapped over Henry. She had jumped out and taken a turn with the bow line around a cleat and had tiptoed up the ladder before he was free of it. Then she was down again, her round face pink with excitement, her ponytail swishing, her eyes sparkling. "Hurry up," she whispered. "They're talking about alligators."

He would have seen at once if he had not known before that the big, easy, commanding man was her father. His wide burned face, under his curly gray hair, was pleasant but the jaw and mouth were strong as a bulldog's.

Under his bushy eyebrows his eyes were hard blue. His clean white pants, his fine blue shirt, his heavy rubber-soled white shoes, and his blue socks looked rich and rare. He was unbelievably unlike the two meager dark men he was talking to, with their worn clothes and their lean, silent faces. Both held the cigarettes he had given them delicately in their long fingers and turned a little away to smoke. Lounging against posts, they listened politely, never meeting each other's eyes.

Behind Agatha's father was his shining expensive yacht on which a thin young man in starched white, with glasses on his beaky nose, was polishing up the brass by the wheel. Henry sat over on the stringpiece of the wharf, crouching away from anyone's eyes. Agatha stood shielding him.

Mr. Ward said, "Here, I can prove that alligator I saw was at least eight feet—Frank, bring me those photographs on my stateroom table—and there were at least three smaller ones. I heard this rustling," his big voice went on enthusiastically, as if he were talking to a lot more people than just these two. "I was getting the camera set for a picture of an eagle's nest in a tree, waiting for the eagle. I was up on the seat of the dinghy. So then I looked down and here was this alligator coming out along a muddy trail to go across the stream. But my boat was in the way so he had to go around it. And how I know he was longer than eight feet was, he was longer than the boat as he went past it. So I just swung the camera down and took him, not thinking about distance or light or anything, and look what I got. That to me is one of the darndest pictures I ever took in my life! Look at that. And that. When he was gone I waited and, by George, down the mud bank slid three more. Nothing like him. Maybe three feet and a half. Maybe four. What do you think?"

He passed the pictures over to Dillon and the dockman who held them carefully, peering at them together. "Well, I declare you're right," the dockman said. "Clear, ain't they? You was shorely right on top of him. Eight foot. Maybe eight and a half. Long time since I seen a big one like that. You, Arlie?"

Henry slid his eye around to look over and up at Dillon. Dillon murmured something but he looked longest at what must have been the photographs of the smaller 'gators.

Dillon said, "Sure got good pictures. Now I wonder if I don't know just about the place this musta been. Up in Whitewater Bay, just about the fifth channel marker, there's a slough to the left that's deeper when you shove through the mangroves . . ."

Agatha's father was delighted. "No, no, you're wrong. Nothing so easy as that. You must take me for a tourist. Ha—ha! You've got to admit I know these lower 'glades just about as well as any of you natives. I'll tell you exactly. You know, you can get up through Whitewater Bay to the cutoff into the Little Shark. There's no channel marked but you've got about three and a half feet. Then you get eight feet in the Little Shark. Well, you follow on up toward Tarpon Bay until the Shark comes into the Little Shark. I left the big boat there and went on in the dink with an outboard. I'd seen birds flying in there and I'd always wanted to find a small rookery and take some real pictures, which I did for a couple of days, coming back to the big boat nights. But it was up the south fork. Then beyond there, I saw an eagle tree. There was a pond, where the 'gators were going. See? I'll bet you there's hardly a man in the Ten Thousand Islands but me knows it."

Dillon handed him back the pictures. "You got me on that one. Sure take good pictures."

Mr. Ward's big laugh boomed out proudly. "Glad you think so," he said. "I must go and show these to the ranger. I'll see you."

"See you around, Mr. Ward," the men murmured politely. Agatha ran down the ladder to her boat. Henry slipped quietly to a lower step and sat rigid, listening. Dillon and the dockman stood finishing their cigarettes.

Henry heard the dockman murmur quietly, "Three at three and a half."

"Maybe four," Dillon murmured. You could hardly hear them at all. "Good enough."

The dockman said, "Tonight?"

Dillon's feet in his worn sneakers moved almost soundlessly up the dock. His voice said, "I'll see."

The dockman waited, humming in the sunshine, before he moved up the dock to the shady door of the big marine supply place where men came and went.

Henry slid down to Agatha on the float. "You know what he'll do?" he whispered violently.

"Who?"

"Dillon. He's going to go and shoot those alligators. Not the big one. It's no use for a skin. The little ones."

"But he can't! They won't let him—"

"Who's going to stop him? They won't know a thing. He gets $3.75 a foot for them up in Tampa. I bet he hangs around here just to listen to people telling about the big 'gators they saw. Or the dockman tells him."

"You could tell the ranger."

"He wouldn't believe me. They couldn't follow him."

She looked at him over her shoulder, her round face thoughtful. Suddenly, seeming older and even wiser than he would ever be, she said, "What's the good of worrying about it then?"

Henry burst out, "Because I hate him, that's why. He killed my alligator. All guys like him—I hate 'em. I'd do anything. . . ."

She said coolly, "But there isn't a thing you can do," and ran up the ladder and left him to his bitterness.

Her father's voice sounded up on the dock again. Henry stared blindly over at Dillon's boat. If he could get over there and wreck it, put sand in the engine, break things, it would be exactly what he felt like. But tomorrow they'd put him on the bus.

He heard Agatha's young voice chirping at him in excitement from the dock and went up the ladder slowly. Mr. Ward was there, talking to the ranger. The dockman was there, listening and watching, the way he always did, Henry thought.

Agatha shouted, "The turtles are coming ashore at Middle Cape Beach in the moonlight, to lay their eggs. Daddy's going to get some photographs, with flashlights. Maybe some raccoons will try to steal the eggs. I asked him to take you, too. He hasn't said 'no' yet. Come on, Daddy. Here he is. Here's Henry. His name is Henry Albert Bunks—he has to go home tomorrow—he wants to go awfully and I haven't had anybody to play with since we got here."

Under the man's suddenly piercing eyes Henry had to stand up and flush and stammer. He knew exactly, from the man's straight gaze, what he himself looked like—still scrawny, still insignificant, his hair too long, his eyes hungry in his sober face. But what he did not expect was the warmth that came after, as if the man looked deeper into him than all of these others could, and smiled, seeing something to respect. But he only said mildly, "Well now, honey, maybe the people that Henry's staying with might not like it if he stayed out as late as we're likely to."

"Please Daddy, please," she said, patting at his arm. "He wants to, terribly."

Henry could only nod.

The dockman, listening as usual, turned his expressionless eyes toward Henry. His nose was crooked in his face as seamed and brown as if the wrinkles had been cut in with a dirty knife. One eyelid was droopy. Half his upper teeth were gone. Henry wouldn't trust him any more than he would Dillon—less. The dockman said, "This the young feller I'm goin' to drive up to Homestead t'morrer, to catch the Miamer bus, ain't it?"

Agatha said, "But Daddy, but Daddy, that's tomorrow. This is tonight. He'd never have a chance like this again."

Her father patted the hand working at his sleeve. "What time were you planning to start in the morning?"

"I figured we'd get goin' about ha-past se'm."

"That's all right then. You tell him where he's staying. He'll be waiting on the dock here when you come. He can sleep on board. That suit you, honey? Come on board, Henry. Frank, how about some pop and cookies? I think we'd better plan to shove off as soon as we can get going, to be there before sunset."

If the dockman looked at him crookedly, Henry did not care. He felt as if his breath had almost left him for good.

An hour later when they cast off, he was hanging with Agatha over the bridge rail, trying not to look as wildly excited and elated as he felt. The big boat—with all its shining gadgets, its decks and deckhouse, the fine chairs and cushions, its polished metal and varnished wood and all the amazing secrets of its elegant compact staterooms below, the sitting room in the deck house, the flowered curtains, wicker chairs, ash trays, games, books even, and the wonderful small galley like a jeweler's window gleaming dark gold colored, with Sam the cook like a bigger jewel among the silvery pots and

81

pans—backed out slowly into the current. Mr. Ward, the wheel in his big hands as the engines thuttered and idled, watched the water, watched to stern, and watched where he was going as he brought it around in the boiling churn and smother of its own wake. The white bow slowly swung true, between the outgoing channel markers, to its course.

Henry found himself looking over and down into Dillon's familiar anchored boat, at his wiry back. He was stowing things away and did not look up. The dinghy lay alongside, loaded with stuff covered with a tarpaulin. "He's going off with my alligator skin," Henry thought raging. There was nothing to stop him. If he could jump over there now, Henry thought, leave all this unnatural magnificence, be there, as much of a man as Dillon, as strong, as crafty, he would—he would . . .

They were surging splendidly out to sea, past green islands of mangroves like bouquets—out to the green, clear, beautiful water, trailing a wake as white as the gulls that flew with them or the white birds on long legs, the egrets and the great white herons that rose from the islands, rose and leveled off and swerved away under the blue afternoon sky. It was unbelievable, Henry thought. He had never had a dream like this.

The low land moved away slowly along the far right hand as the green small waves crushed steadily under the bow. The salt wind blew at them from the southern horizon where white clouds stood like snowy hills. Mr. Ward showed him on the big chart just where they were going. That was East Cape now, pointed on the map, only a streak of green and yellow land edged with a little white. Mr. Ward took them in nearer. "If you look sharp, you can see Guy Bradley's grave," he said pointing. "More like a heap of stones.

"They killed him not far from Flamingo, when it was a bigger village than it ever has been since. Mr. Flagler was going to make this the jumping-off place for the Overseas Railway to Key West. He thought Flamingo would amount to a lot more than Miami, then. Of course, the engineers found that wasn't practical. But Guy Bradley's father brought his family down from Lake Worth to be the first real estate man in Flamingo. And the Audubon Society, which was fighting the people who sold egret plumes for ladies' hats in New York, got a bill passed making the killing of birds for their plumes a crime. Young Guy Bradley wasn't like these tough guys down here. He played the violin and read books. But he could use a gun and he wasn't afraid of them.

"One day he heard that a bunch of men he knew had shot up an egret rookery. They were off Flamingo in a schooner. So he went out alone in his light sailing boat, ran up to the schooner and laid hold of her rail to go aboard. He said, 'I hear you boys have got some plumes here and I've come for them.'

"There was a man from up West Palm Beach way standing at the rail and he took out his gun and shot right down at Guy Bradley, so that the bullet angled down from his shoulder into his heart. He dropped down in his boat dead. They shoved it off and let the tide take it. Later they found it grounded among the mangroves and his body in it.

"They were a tough lot of people then," Mr. Ward said. "They got away with murder. What do you think of that, Henry?"

Henry looked up at him. They were standing by the rail together. Young Agatha was steering, following the channel markings, her legs curled around the legs of the tall stool, her ponytail stiff with purpose. "There's a lot of people now that still do," he said.

The man turned to look down at him, unsmiling. "It's tough when you've had to learn it at your age, Henry," he said. "But once you've learned it, you don't have to learn it twice."

Henry thought that over slowly and the man watched him thinking. He said soberly, "Yes, that's true." It would be something to remember a long time. It made him feel as he met the older man's steady look that they were neither older nor younger but men of an equal understanding in a hard world.

He went on looking at the chart. There was Flamingo. There was Whitewater Bay beyond a canal, inland, and the area of jumbled water and islands that marked the end of the great curving expanse that led northward, marked THE EVERGLADES.

Mr. Ward turned and said, "Hey, honey, think it's time we let Henry here take his trick at the wheel?"

The western sky was beginning to stream with great

84

pink rays, making the rushing sea before his bow greener and more glowing than jewels filled with light. The big boat answered to his least pressure on the wheel. His wrists were iron as he held her steady. His legs were long and strong. Wind blew his hair. He was Henry Albert Bunks, commanding the most wonderful ship in the finest sea in the best and most beautiful of worlds.

Behind them in the open-windowed deckhouse, Sam, the cook, was setting the table for a dinner of broiled fish, baked potatoes, hot biscuits, and heaven only knew what else—the smells of which he began deeply, luxuriantly, ravenously, to inhale.

Cape Sable by Moonlight

A FTER dinner, while there was still light and it was too early to go ashore, Henry looked eagerly at the bird photographs in color Mr. Ward had been making. He was glad he recognized so many birds and could name them: the delicate blue-gray Louisiana heron, the snowy egret bristling with fine white plumes over its black legs and yellow feet—"little golden gloves," Mr. Ward said—the great wood stork with its black wing tips, balancing with its down-curved bill on some small tree, and the least blue heron. But he had not seen the huge white pelican or the roseate spoonbill or the glossy ibis, and he stared in bewilderment at all the pictures of the little shore birds, the sandpipers and terns and turnstones. Agatha knew them, every one.

The pictures Mr. Ward was proudest of, he could tell, were a whole set taken of nesting snowy egrets—the parent birds' feathers shining in the sun, the baby birds' queer fuzzy heads bobbing out of the untidy stick nest. "Took me nearly two days to get those feeding pictures," Mr. Ward told him. "I had to fix up a kind of blind because the birds were so shy. Look at this one. The baby's head is way down the old one's throat. Feeding. Look at this. I like this shot, looking straight up into a flock dropping down on the nests from high up, coming back from the feeding ground. All these years I've been wanting to get these rookery pictures but I never got the right chance until I found this rookery on my own."

Henry said to him solemnly, "I think those must be the best bird pictures anybody ever took in this world. There's lots of things to learn."

He breathed a long sigh. Mr. Ward laughed and patted his shoulder. "I'll tell you one thing, nobody ever learns a thing unless he really wants to. Hey, the light's almost gone. We got to get ashore."

Flashlights showed them the narrow old dock that took them ashore at Middle Cape, on the long beach. Everyone carried armloads of the gear that Frank brought in the dinghy. Mr. Ward's cameras came first, of course, with flashlights, lenses, tripods, boxes of film. There were blankets to spread on the beach for the younger ones to lie and doze on if the waiting was long, and folding chairs and mosquito dope and thermos jugs of coffee. How could anybody even have so many things, Henry wondered. In the old days, he had been told, men landed here when the turtles came ashore and filled buckets with eggs, turning over the turtles to take them away alive or killing them with hatchets. But for a few pictures you had to have boatloads of stuff.

A strong wind was blowing in from the sea, over the dim unknown land. The beach whitened as they walked it under the moon that was beginning to rise above the dark hissing sea, streaked with long quivery trails of moon-fire. Inshore, the little waves were edged with the soft fire of phosphorus that lay in long streaks after a wave had washed and gone, washed and gone. The night was so enormous and so brilliant they could speak only in hushed voices, standing, walking, or staring.

Perhaps it did not matter where they put their things, Mr. Ward said when they had walked so far along the narrow beach edged with dark scrub that the yacht lights were only bright points in the distance. The long V-shaped tracks of turtles that had come ashore in the last few nights were only a little blurred by blowing sand. Others might come in anywhere. They themselves must not get excited and move about or talk, but keep a sharp lookout as far as they could see up and down the long curving beach. There was nothing to do but wait. Agatha and Henry each spread a blanket and a cushion and lay down on them, trying not to wiggle or giggle, their faces turned up, staring high above the moon into the faintly colored outer reaches of the night.

"No mosquitoes," Mr. Ward murmured to them. He was sitting in a folding chair, smoking a cigarette in the hollow of his hand. Frank sat in the sand at his feet. His glasses gleamed in the moonlight as he turned his head on his long neck. No one was more solemnly eager about all this than Frank. He had studied to be a naturalist before he had to take this job. Nobody said anything. There was only the sound of the wind over them and the endless hush and foam of all that restless silvery water under the moony light.

Henry was a little surprised that he was not more excited. It was all so strange, but he was so comfortable. This must be what happiness was, he was thinking, not to be anxious about anything, to be so comfortable, to love the night so, to feel safe. The little girl had turned over on her side and was completely quiet. Her father stooped and spread a sweater over her shoulders. He was peering down at Henry, who turned his head slowly and smiled. The men's voices murmured a word or two now and then. Henry slept.

He woke abruptly, knowing he had slept for a long time. A hand joggled his shoulder insistently. When he stared upward, blinking, the high moon was curving down again. The light was changed. The sea was darker. Only the edges of the incoming waves were marked with the moonlight that glared whitely on the long beach.

Mr. Ward whispered to him, "One turtle's come up

and has dug her hole in the soft sand. There's two more coming in now. Look down there." He saw two black blotches slowly coming in from the waves, pushing up the sand. Agatha was awake now, squeezing his hand. They got up, walked slowly westward, carrying all the things.

Frank said, "You can't disturb a turtle once she's started laying, not if you pulled her flippers."

Mr. Ward whispered, "See there in the soft sand back of the ridge of weed. The first turtle has stopped digging her hole with her back flippers. She's been quiet now more than half an hour. There's another coming ashore beyond her."

Henry could just make out the black head and the shape in the moonlight, like a half-covered rock. Mr. Ward moved forward. Then the flashlight popped and lighted everything for its brief second with its white, theatrical glare. He fixed his camera and it popped again, until their staring eyes were blinded.

He was back with them at once, murmuring, "She didn't move. She hardly blinked. Bring up the blankets and stuff. We can settle right here. I want more pictures of her when she's covering her eggs."

The boy and the girl lay flat on their blankets again, listening to Frank's hushed voice, as he sat cross-legged by Mr. Ward's chair. "Loggerheads," he said. "Not as good to eat as green turtles. The eggs are all right. They make good cake. But the whites won't cook hard. These turtles are nearly three feet long, maybe 150 pounds. They've been coming to lay their eggs on beaches around the gulf and the Caribbean for thousands and thousands of years. They say they always come back to the place where they were hatched.

The words hung in Henry's quieting mind. How long was a thousand years? One night like this was a long, long time. What Henry said began to be mixed up with his doze. He thought what it would be like to be an old turtle with a beak and a wrinkled neck and great heavy plated shells, living and sleeping long months on the green swaying surface of the sea, diving and coming up often to breathe, moving on some regular course from the beach where he was born, out to sea, to the feeding grounds, to find a mate, then back to the same beach, year after year—to think of the sunny, green, lifting and falling waves . . . Henry slept.

Once he was startled awake to hear, far away, a thin, long-drawn-out, high scream that made him shiver. The watchful men heard it. He heard Mr. Ward's voice with a sound of excitement in it. The small girl slept soundly.

The moon's glare slowly curved westward, changing all the shadows and darkening them. The bright waters dimmed. Henry forced his sleepy eyes open to watch the slow dark shape of another turtle pushing across the beach beyond. He heard birds flying low overhead, croaking. "Night heron," Frank murmured. Insects creaked in the tall, coarse grass. Crabs crawled in the wet sand. The night was crammed and teeming with life, he thought. Under the waves, perhaps millions of fish lay half sleeping, half moving. He had never known a night could be like this.

The flashlight awakened him at least twice more. Mr. Ward bent to him, "She's leaving. Keep an eye on Agatha, Frank. Come along, Henry, quiet."

There was still a little distance of moon-white sand between them, and the turtle was moving slower than ever, as if exhausted, toward the sea. Mr. Ward had his camera ready, the flashlight lifted. Henry squeezed his arm violently. "There's something there," he whispered. They waited, stock still.

Clouds moved slowly across the lower moon. A shadow covered them. At its darkest, they heard something digging where the turtle had left its nest. There was nothing to see but shadow. Then moonlight caught sand spurting. Shadow lingered there, then moved.

The muscles of the man's arm were suddenly tight under Henry's fingers. His arm jerked up. The flash exploded. Light flashed back out of flat green eyes, glaring in a snarling black head. Even as the dark blinded them, their eyes retained, like the camera, the image of white teeth in the open snarling mouth, the curve of a lean body over the white nest of eggs, the long tail. "Panther," Mr. Ward shouted. "A black panther. I got him." They heard the leap. Bushes crashed. Then came the scream, right from there—the full-throated, wild, defiant cat screech that brought out the gooseflesh on Henry's back as if he heard a woman being murdered.

"I saw it, I saw it," Agatha was squealing at his elbow.

"I woke up in time. A black panther. Wasn't he marvelous? Wasn't it marvelous, Henry?" Mr. Ward was thumping them both on the back. "I got it. A swell shot. I know it was. Now let's get a shot of the eggs and cover them right up. I bet that panther's too scared to come back for a couple of nights." He was so excited he nearly dropped the flashlight and they forgot to be quiet, until afterward.

Then they went back in the loaded dinghy, from the wharf to the boat.

"I'm hungry. Wake up, Sam. Got some sandwiches?" Mr. Ward said on deck. "What a night. Hey, Agatha, did you really see him?"

Henry said, "Gee Mr. Ward, wasn't that terrific? I bet nobody ever got a picture like that."

"Luck," Mr. Ward kept saying over and over, staring back to the narrow dark line of the beach. "Start the engine, Frank. We might as well get home." He was at the wheel. "It's still bright enough to see the markers. But you better turn on the headlight. Get below to Frank's other bunk, Henry. You remember you've got to be on the dock at seven thirty tomorrow morning. Sam'll give you your breakfast. You say good-bye to Henry now, honeybug. You'll be sound asleep in the morning when he goes. And I will, too, you can bet. We had fun, didn't we, Henry? It was great having you. Hope we'll get together again some time."

Henry tried to thank him but Mr. Ward was absent-minded, watching his course intently as they went forward

at a careful speed. Henry said, "I'd rather sleep up here."
Nobody paid any attention to him. He curled up on a
bench by the rail, in one of the blankets. Sometimes he
dozed. Then he woke himself with a violent effort. He
could not afford to waste the last of this in sleep. If he
could stay awake, maybe he could still think of something he could do before seven o'clock in the morning.

Once in a while Frank took the wheel and Mr. Ward
paced and kept a sharp lookout. Once in a while he
heard their voices muttering as they passed a channel
marker whitened by their search light, and they changed
their course a little. The night, the sea, rushed by them
to the steady surging of the boat. The moon was setting
red over a black land, black water. High up and eastward, there were stars.

Ahead Henry saw the lights of Flamingo—lonely road
lights, night lights in buildings—as the channel within
the Keys opened up beyond. Henry was not sleepy at all
now. There it was before him, the end of all this amazing
time. Its speed checked, the yacht moved forward slowly
toward its berth. They went by anchored boats. They
went by Arlie Dillon's boat, dark. Henry looked over and
down into the familiar cockpit. He could just make out
that the cabin door was open, as it was when Dillon slept
aboard. His loaded dinghy, on a short line, heaved to
their bow wave, ready to go at the first gleam of light.

Henry kept on staring. A hand clutched his knee.
It was Agatha. "You aren't going back, are you, Henry?"
she whispered. They were coming into their dock. The

engines were silenced. Frank jumped with the bow line. Mr. Ward's big figure was ready at the stern. The big boat settled creaking and rubbing at the bumpers. They heard the last of the churned water slapping the pilings. Mr. Ward yawned tremendously. "A good run, Frank," he said. "I'll leave you to make fast. Goodnight."

Frank said, "Goodnight, sir," busy on quiet feet with the lines, busy with the deck things. The girl stood in shadow as the boy still crouched on his bench.

"No," he said softly.

"What are you going to do, then?" she whispered.

It took him a long time. "I guess—I'll just have to borrow your pram," he said finally.

"When'll you bring it back?"

"I don't know how I can get it back."

"Where are you going?"

He wet his lips and swallowed. Once he said it, then he would have to do it. He nodded out there, to Dillon's boat.

He felt the intensity with which she turned and stared out there into the darkness, making up her mind what he meant. There were no sounds from the land. Everybody was asleep, the people in the motels, the people in the trailers, the rangers in their houses, the men on boats. Her father must already have been in his bed. Frank was quiet somewhere, down below.

"When?" she asked.

"He'll go out at daylight. It might as well be now."

"I'll take you."

"All right," he said, took a long breath, and stood up. It was settled.

She slipped down the ladder in her bare feet ahead of him, to the float where her pram lay, its sail tidily rolled. "Let go the bow line and get in," she whispered and sat in the stern with her short paddle. He stood by the mast. The little craft poked forward gingerly. He felt her paddle push and heard it drip, push, and drip. It wasn't very far.

He leaned over and fended off the dinghy so the two boats would not bump. The tarpaulin was tucked under a couple of big cans. He loosened it. As he got over, making no sound, he pushed at the pram with his left foot. He felt it leave him. He heard the water gurgle as she thrust in her paddle and brought it around. He did not wait to see her slipping away.

The whole problem was to get under the tarpaulin with no sound, to find a place to lie without moving a box or jarring a can. In the pitch-black underneath, he inched and wedged his body around things, waiting minutes, as long as he could, before trying to shift a hip jammed against a sharp corner or a shoulder cramped against a thwart. He had to have air, too, and with infinite pains lifted a stiff corner of the tarpaulin toward the stern and got his face where he could breathe.

He could put his head on his arm and try to forget what was poking into his back. Excitement, dread, determination, sleeplessness all suddenly gave way to utter exhaustion. He slept and dreamed. He did not wake until a burst of sound exploded just ahead of him and he was jounced awake, rolled and jarred, as the dinghy's bow line was jerked tight in the wash of water when the big fishboat plowed out, roared, was turned, went away from there on some watery course he could not imagine. The first light warmed the tarpaulin over his face.

Beyond Whitewater Bay

As he lay in darkness under the tarpaulin with the boat booming ahead, he became aware of a kind of hollow echoing rush and wash of sound from each side, very near. He remembered the map. There was a narrow canal into Whitewater Bay from the docks at Flamingo. Their wake must be trailing its yellowed waves between muddy banks, under trees from which the rushing echo came back. At Whitewater Bay, if they turned to the right, they would get to the docks at Coot Bay, on the main road into the park. But he was pretty sure that Dillon's intention now was to have nothing to do with any park people, but to go left and go through that more or less open water of Whitewater Bay. If they followed carefully the channel markings, boats could move through this shortcut to the Gulf of Mexico instead of going all the way around the three pointed capes and beaches of Cape Sable. Many boats passed that way from east to west, the big park service boat, boats of commercial fishermen, and any number of small boats and park visitors. They moved slowly among the shallows and the tall green mangroves, or anchored in some leafy corner, intent on their fishing lines.

Dillon would go past them all at the legal top speed, hardly turning his head. It would just not be long before he would slow down to creep as quietly as possible into some unmarked stream, hidden beyond mangroves. Henry remembered the phrase, "the Little Shark cutoff," and beyond that where the Shark River joined the Little Shark there was a narrow branch—he had no way of knowing what it meant. It lead down to a bewildering region of ponds and wandering streams that few could follow without getting lost. Dillon knew it all exactly.

The sun had risen. Henry began to feel it hot on the tarpaulin over his face. His side was aching and one foot was prickling asleep. However, in the jarring sway of their speed he managed to shift a little and even pushed a corner of the heavy covering back so that the cooler air found his hot forehead. He was still too uncomfortable to doze and he was aware, as he had been from the moment he had left the shelter of the yacht, that the familiar habit of anxiety, of timidity, and of dread was clutching at his throat again. What on earth was he doing here? What would Dillon do to him? He began to wonder why he had not simply told Mr. Ward that he was sure Dillon would go after those alligators and let Mr. Ward warn the rangers. Yet even here he was glad that he was not on the bus going home.

The sound of water dragged along the muddy canal banks ceased. The engines ahead picked up speed in what was surely wide-open water. The bow was gradually turning in a long curve to the left, with the laden dinghy slapping heavily behind.

Now he began to forget even his anxiety because the sun was really getting high and he lay curled in a sweat bath of heat like a stifling blanket. The perspiration tickled and trickled and ran down his body. His face was stinging with it. He tried to hold the loose end of the tarpaulin up, to let more air in, but in time his arms tired. Sun scorched the black stuff over him until he thought his skin was almost burning. The only relief came when the boat ahead, slackening its speed, moved snapping and rustling under low boughs and leaves where the sun was cut off by shade.

It did not cool him. They were soon out in the open sun again, as if, emerging from some shortcut between mangroves, Dillon had found a deeper water course where the sun blasted down.

Henry was growing dizzy. He could not stand it. He pushed back the tarpaulin recklessly from his face and breathed. The air was cooler but his head was in full sun and red wheels exploded under his smarting eyelids.

The engine ahead had increased its beat. Now and then spray from the bow came over, rattling like shot across the tarpaulin, striking his burning face with wet. With one convulsive effort he pushed himself backward into the stern from among the crannies of the boxes, heaved the tarpaulin away from over him, and sat up in full sight. Spray dashed his burning face and body with coolness. His panting diminished. Ahead of the dinghy, beyond the towline, the boat's stern was low in the boiling water among the boiling mist and yellow spray of its going. He could hardly read the faded letters, TRIXIE, MARCO. He stared transfixed at the back of Arlie Dillon, lounging at the tiller in his usual position, knee up, arm steady, eyes fixed ahead.

They were speeding along a narrow stream of brown-stained water between high trees, the arched roots, the dark green leaves of the eternal mangroves. Through the screen of leaves sometimes, if he turned his head, he could see the bright spatters of sunshine on some bent trunk far within. Yet, but for this line of sun they seemed to follow, the trees stood huge and dark and shadowy. Nothing but mangroves.

The boy's hair blew back from his wet red forehead. He sat on the narrow stern seat bolt upright, clutching hard with both hands. His body did not ache. He breathed deep. But his eyes were fixed in growing concern on the quiet back of the man ahead.

The waterway was narrowing in. The deep chocolate water grew yellow with shallows. The man cut the boat's speed until its roaring was almost idling. Ahead there seemed to be a solid wall of leaves and no water at all.

The bow poked slowly among the leaves that scraped its heavy awning. There was a gleam of water ahead, an almost invisible passage. The dinghy scraped the mud. Dillon was standing, steering with his knee, watching the water alongside. His head turned to watch forward and then back.

Perhaps suddenly, or out of the corner of his eye, he caught sight of something strange in the stern of the dinghy. He stood and turned and stared full into Henry's reddened, shrinking face.

Dillon's eyes in his stony face widened until the whites gleamed about the dark pupils. His nostrils were flaring holes. The boat, violently, ran into the mud and stopped. He half fell, but cut his engine. Henry was flung forward on the tarp. As he picked himself up, the grim-faced man hauled on the dinghy's painter. There was water enough to bring it up with a rush alongside.

His hand reached Henry's arm and, with one dis-locating jerk, brought him aboard on the floor. When he got up, Dillon slapped him on the jaw twice with his open hand. The shock knocked Henry down again. He could have stayed there, stinging cheek on the boards, eyes blinking at Dillon's dirty sneaker. But he scrambled up to brace his back against the awning post. Instantly, Dillon's open hand snaked out and struck. He was falling. By sheer instinct his fists clutched the post, as if there were nothing below him but emptiness, so that when he opened his eyes he was still hanging on, half standing up. His nose, half his face, was numb. His wiping hand showed bright red with blood. His blood. The beginning of a sob jerked at his stomach muscles.

But he did not have to cry. He drew breath deep in his lungs, ground his teeth, blinked, held on, until the fire in his head cleared a little. He did not have to cry because he was not sorry for himself. He was furious. Rage cleared his head, stiffened his jaw, his grip, his whole body.

"Don't you hit me again!" he croaked.

Dillon said, between his teeth, "I do' know what's to stop me killin' you."

He looked nine feet high. Perhaps he would kill him.

Henry said, "You won't get three dollars a foot for my skin in Tampa."

He could loosen his cramped grip from the post. Dillon looked at him, looked around him quickly, looked back. "What do you think you're doin' here anyway, you filthy little rat?"

Henry's head was ringing. His nose was swelling and stinging so that he could hardly breathe through it. But he could stand up on his own feet. He said, "I told you I wouldn't go home."

Dillon's mouth was relaxing into disgust. "You're the last thing alive I'd want around," he said. "A dog-gone useless kid. I haven't got time to bother with you."

Henry said nothing but he felt better.

"I suppose you figured you'd get out here so far I

wouldn't stop to take you back. Well, you're right. But I'll tell you. You been figurin' like a kid. From here on, you gonta work like a man."

Henry wiped at the blood on his face. "OK," he said.

Dillon moved to the tiller. "Get over the side then and shove the bow off the mud." He reversed the engine. Henry went overboard in one leap. His feet went down in feather-soft mud. Muddy water closed over his head. When he kicked out, his foot hit a slimy sunken branch, but it was enough to get his gasping head above water. The bow was a solid wall over him. "Push," Dillon yelled. "Get your back into it."

So as long as he was braced against the bow he could push, but it wasn't much. Dillon shut off the engine and pushed from the bow with a long pole. The bow tipped. Henry pushed and floundered. The bow gave. Dillon leaped back and reversed his engine. The boat slid away, came back, passed slowly. "The dinghy," Dillon shouted to him. "Hurry up."

Floundering that was part swimming got him desperately to the smaller boat. He hung and heaved, lifted himself by one leg. The rail scraped his stomach as he rolled over onto the tarpaulin where it was enough to lie with water streaming off him, his chest pumping, his back and legs twitching with exhaustion. Dillon let him alone.

At half speed the boat was following a crooked channel between mangroves that opened out, or more often, met overhead. Sometimes branches scraped the awning.

Sometimes leaves trailed along his back. In him deeper than aches and pains, relief was rising. The first shock, at least, was over. And he was here.

Shadows were cool over them when Dillon switched off his ignition, letting the heavy boat slide forward a little under arched branches. Its bow was cushioned easily in mud. The dinghy kept moving until it nuzzled the stern ahead and was quiet.

Henry watched Dillon go forward and run a line around a tree trunk. Water lay deep chocolate brown among the roots to each side and ahead. The boat's side rubbed against roots covered with little shells and shiny green growths moving with the gentle water. Henry looked up, as Dillon did, to see nothing but green heavy overhead—no sky, and only a little moving spatter of sun through the leaky roof.

"Fold up that tarp," Dillon said to him. When he got the thing off he saw the demijohns of water, a box of supplies, the axe, the hatchet, and a lantern, between which he had angled his body so uncomfortably all night. Now Dillon passed him other things to stow where he pointed—fish rods and reels of line, a box with the frying pan and the coffee pot, a bottle of whiskey, the net, the small anchor, two cotton blankets, an iron rod. Dillon passed him a paddle. When he had stowed everything else in the cabin, locked the door, pocketed the key, he stepped into the stern of the dinghy carrying his .30-30 rifle and motioned to Henry to cast off. Then Dillon stood, and with the long pole with the widened end feeling out the bottom, he deftly pushed the heavy laden boat backward along the way they had come.

When the alley of brown water was wide enough to turn the boat in, Henry looked back. He could see no sign at all of the bigger boat behind the screening trees. He could not even imagine how Dillon could possibly find the place again—it was so like everything else. There was a dead tree just about at the entrance of the boat's hiding place, with something like a black rag hanging from it. It may have been a snake's discarded skin. But that was all.

Where they went now, among the unending mangroves, Henry saw that the water was so shallow over the mud and sandbanks covered with scrub that nothing could go here but a boat like this one—flat, and even with its burden, no deeper than a few inches—or, perhaps, an alligator.

The mangroves were drawing away from the muddy banks covered with a thick yellow weed, where thousands of tiny crabs ran to their holes. The sun was strong in a sky open over them again. Under its glare a mass of half-bare tree trunks lifted gray, as if they had been blasted, but not knocked down, in some forgotten hurricane. There were curious lumps of sticks and things among the branches. And as Dillon's steady pole with its little sound of dripping and its gentle push took them forward, Henry saw big black birds flying and moving about the trees. He heard their cawing. The sun gleamed on their feathers as if they dripped ink. The sky was bluer because of their blackness and the whiteness of leaves plastered with bird guano.

"Crows," Dillon said.

"What's happened?" Henry stared at the tall bushes, the tree shapes drawing nearer. The lumps of stuff were hundreds of birds' nests made of sticks. But there were no birds overhead save the inky great crows. Now there was a stench. Broken eggshells littered the ground. He saw a snake, two or three snakes, looped among the twigs. The nests were empty except for blowing feathers or crows lighting and straddling about, picking at what he could not see. Dillon wrinkled his nose at the smell and spat into the water.

"How do you like that?" he exclaimed. "You see what happened? Some guy was around here with one of those fancy cameras, taking those color pitchers that they're crazy about. Two-three days. The eggs in the nests was about ready to hatch. See what happens? Any fool oughta know. Anybody fussin' around like these camera guys— set 'em up here, set 'em up there, climb the trees, crash around underneath gettin' the light right, monkeyin' with all those gadgets—why, them plume birds leave ever' last nest. They keep on flyin' around, try to come in, get scared off—why, you know, them eggs can't be left alone more than a little more than an hour before the unhatched birds begin to die. Two-three hours, most of them's dead. These guys fuss around a coupla days. Next time, they can't see what's become of the birds. But the crows do. Before night they come flockin' in, breakin' the shells, eatin' the eggs. Ever' one. An' what the crows don't get the snakes an' raccoons and the marsh rats finish up, and the ants march in and clean. All gone an' wasted for nuthin'. In the old days, when we—when a rookery got shot up, it was for money. It did some good to somebody. Now if anybody was fool enough to try to come in and shoot up a rookery, even a little one like this that nobody but a few people knew was here—why, he'd get fined and jailed. Even though there's nobody anymore wants to buy plumes. But a man with money enough to buy expensive cameras, he can come in here and ruin a rookery just as quick as if he took after the birds with clubs, and ever'body looks an' says, 'What pretty pitchers.' Makes you sick."

Henry sat hunched up sorrowfully in the bow, sorrowful for the little birds, aghast at what his good friend Mr. Ward had done. He couldn't have had any idea. Henry remembered every one of those pictures—the birds with their fine haze of feathers. Now they were all gone away and there was nothing left of the baby birds but the bad smell.

It was frightening to think of all the things that went on like this here, away from the cruel things of cities. It was frightening to think how many kinds of men there were in the world, every one with a different idea of what was good and what was not good. It made him heavy with a new kind of sadness that was not for himself at all.

Beyond, grasses grew alongside, higher than Dillon's

head. The water was a little deeper again. It opened out in a shallow kind of pond where dragonflies darted and mosquitoes sung about their ears. Ahead, but inland a little among bushes, he saw a tall tree topped with a great bunch of stuff like twigs and weeds hardly interwoven, bushels of stuff with dead branches holding it on.

They went past slowly enough to stare and turn and look high over. A great brown bird came swinging on quiet wings. He saw the flash of white head, the great familiar hooked beak. It dropped to the branch above the nest and stood there motionless, a square-shouldered, white-legged, heavy bird.

"It's an eagle," Henry said, breathlessly. "It's a bald eagle. I've seen it!" Dillon hardly nodded. The great bird let them go by without seeming to notice them. His hard round eyes were watching something far away. It was the eagle tree that Mr. Ward had showed him the picture of, just where he had said it was. They were going straight to the place where he had seen the alligators.

There was nothing he could do about it.

The boat went on with its steady gliding. The sun went over. The water in the shallow stream glittered. Tall grasses stood high again. Strange birds called and cried and unseen insects zeed. Buzzards slowly tilted high. The tips of their wings against the dazzle were inky fingers feeling the air currents. Ducklike birds hurried along the mud. There were muddy shadows of fish in the water, and dancing dragonflies.

The world was sunny, airy, brimming and vibrating

with life in every sort of darting, gleaming, calling, soaring form. And he was all right, so far.

"Dillon," he spoke up, facing him, "I haven't had
anything to eat since last night. I've got to have something to eat right now."

Dillon looked down at him as he poled, with no
expression at all in his fixed face. He shoved the pole
once hard, to keep it still by the bank, and jerked his
chin at the tin box that had gouged Henry's back all
night. "Well," he said sitting down in the stern, "then
let's eat."

Alligator Crossing

T HEY had eaten store-bought sandwiches of thick
bread and ham done up in a shiny paper, and bananas, and had taken big swigs of cold coffee out of a
bottle and gone on, sometimes paddling in a winding
stream. Mangrove clumps went by and grassy banks set
with scrub. Skinny Louisiana heron blew up and veered
away before them. Kingfishers rattled over, the fat dark
birds like ducks on stilts that Dillon said were "gallinules"
pattered along the muddy banks ahead. Sometimes
Henry stared at the black shoe-polished loops of a water
moccasin lying by a fallen branch, its lidless eye unwink-
ing in its arrowy head. Once Dillon told him to look into
the branches of a bush ahead, just in time to see a long

reddish rope of a water snake unwind itself and plop into the water. "Is it poisonous?" Henry asked.

"Naw. But they're mean," Dillon said in his quiet voice. "Sharp edges to their mouths. Make a mean bite. Just's leave be bitten by a moccasin."

"You been bitten?"

"Be my own fault. Kick them out of the way. 'Course, you got to watch out. They don't give no warning like an ole rattler. They can even strike when they're float-ing coiled on top the water. What you don't want to do, though, is don't never look down an see this pretty white flower opened up an' put down your hand to pick it, because that's ole man cottonmouth coiled up flat with his jaws wide open and bent back—the insides white just like a flower, with his fangs stickin' right up at you."

The waterway widened. Across there was a shelf of mud, crisscrossed with tracks and long scratchings. Be-yond, the grasses grew tall and there were lily pads and yellow lilies Dillon called "bonnets" and lavender water hyacinths, with a track of clear water in the middle that held the color of the sunny sky. Dillon had rested his paddle to look at the mud beside him. "Huh," he snorted and his mouth was creased with satisfaction, "they oughta put up a sign like the one they got on the road into the park for the tourists, says 'Alligator Crossing.'"

"Is that the place?" Henry said. "Where are they?"

Dillon said, "Don't you worry," and picked up his paddle. The boat shoved out among the green water plants of a little pond as dozens of white wings went flapping up and circling off overhead. To the left there was deep shade under a tangle of trees.

"Just about the place I shot my first 'gator," Dillon said with what sounded like cheer, for him. "Me and my daddy and some other men come up someplace like this. I's about your age, on'y not so skinny and no-'count lookin'. Years ago, that was. Water was higher then. You never see anything like the 'gators. Pond was so full of 'gators an' garfish you coulda walked right across on their backs. That's when I killed my first one. Took three days to clean 'em out."

"All of them," Henry said heavily.

"Ever' last one of 'em. Bought my first rifle. I forgot all about it until that guy the other day said . . . an' then I thought to myself, I bet I remembered the very place."

He drove the boat across to the bank under the dark trees. It was a rocky outcrop, with the water or swamp going around it, like a small island. Dillon handed Henry his long swordlike machete and said, "Look out for moccasins now. But get out and haul up the bow a bit and take a coupla turns with the painter around that stump." Henry swished the blade among the weeds with some apprehension before he got out. Dillon stepped ashore with a hatchet in his hand and moved quietly, peering here and there into the coolness under the trees. In the shadow there was a kind of old platform of boughs raised on corner posts, which Dillon shook and approved of. "Some Indian had a camp here," he said. "Maybe froggers. Start gettin' the stuff out of the boat.

And give me the machete. There'll be a coupla moccasins to kill."

Henry moved gingerly back and forth from the boat, heavy laden, in the path of his own making, while Dillon chopped and crashed away on the other side of the rocks. "Only three or four," he called, throwing heavy things into the water beyond.

Everything went on the platform. The water bottles had their own place. With the brightness all about the patch of shadow it was secret and secure and exciting. Dillon pulled out one of the blankets, spread it, and unconcernedly lay down to sleep. "Nothin' to do till dark," he said. "We'll eat cold grub tonight. No good risking a fire, though. The patrol plane comes over long before sunset."

There was no sleepiness in Henry's eyes. "Can I—take the boat an' the paddle?" he said.

Dillon yawned and grunted and was asleep. He had not said, "No."

The flat boat was buoyant with emptiness. Henry shoved it off and stood for a moment with the paddle in his hand, his face turned to the sky. He was completely, entirely, utterly alone. When he looked around him at the green leaves on the pond, the water rippling in the wind that bent the tall yellow grasses beyond the nearer shore, he had in his life never been so filled with sheer, mindless, unutterable delight.

The white birds they had disturbed were feeding again by the farther shore. Two pink birds flew over.

They flew with their necks straight, sticking out funny-shaped bills, wonderful pink birds with deep rosy splashes on their wings. Spoonbill—roseate spoonbill, he thought before he realized it. He was so excited because he had recognized them from the pictures that he nearly fell overboard. Birds—gallinules that he remembered, and coots—were clucking among the lily pads. Overhead a buzzard tilted its black wings and, motionless, rode high up a mounting column of air. There were fish in the water around him, long gray shapes. He thought they were garfish that somebody said the Indians ate.

Presently, full to the brim with happiness, he sat down in the stern and practiced paddling. He got half across. Then he saw a bird and forgot to paddle. It was sitting, black and tan, on one of the scrubby bushes at the water's edge. It had a long snaky neck like those cormorants in the Bay of Florida, but this was longer. It was the snakebird, he remembered. Dillon called it a "water turkey." He waited, perfectly still, and saw the bird dip easily from its branch in a long dive to the water—down into it and disappear. It was swimming down there in the dim weedy water, with the little fish darting. He waited and waited to see it come up, but he couldn't tell if it was that one or another that came flying over and took to another tree.

Everywhere he looked he could see birds, paddling at the water's edge, hanging on the farther reeds, chirring or flying over low and busy, standing on long

legs in the shallows, like a heron over there with its long
sharp beak extended like a lance at the ready. Up there
higher in the sky, birds crisscrossed it with wings floating, turning, dipping, or soaring high—high up like the
buzzard, swinging on the point of one black wing right
against the dazzling breast of a cloud rising up snowy
into the sun.

When he brought his eyes down they were swimming
with too much light. It was as if, from this moment, he
wanted never to move again.

When his eyes cleared he saw two dark bumps of alligator eyes and a smaller bump of a nose moving easily
out from among the lily pads. It was only a little distance
between the eyes. The easy swirl of water behind was the
sculling ridgy tail. It wasn't a big alligator, only about
two foot and a half, about the size of George. He kept
perfectly still as it went by, cocking an eye at his shadow.
The curving mouth smiled a little. The short front legs
hung down foolishly by the bulge of the body. It was just
a small blackish alligator moving across a pond, just
where he belonged—probably looking for a turtle to
crunch on from the other side.

Henry thought about it slowly. Thinking was hard.
Everything that lived here—the alligator, the little fish
and big fish, the turtles, the frogs, the dragonflies—lived
on something else alive that was here, even the green
water plants in the clear brown water. There seemed
to be enough for them all so long as there was enough
freshwater. Only the alligator was not killed and eaten

by anything—except man. But man was different. Man frightened Henry, but not these strange bright living things as intensely alive as he was.

It was so—so nice here. If he could only stay here by himself. It was impossible. There were all the things a boy had to face, just growing up. It looked hard to him in this moment of peace. Yet he'd lived through a lot of things already, he remembered suddenly, as if his life before this was already a long time ago. He was still astonished that he had found his way to this. The idea came to him slowly that perhaps there were things as fine as this waiting for him somewhere that he could not imagine now. He had a new, strong sense of hope that was not a boy's imagining.

But there was this very night facing him with dread. He looked regretfully after the alligator that had caught a turtle by the far bank and had climbed on solid ground to brace his lower jaw while his upper came down hard and crunchy on the squirming turtle's back. He was not indignant at the death of the turtle. That was natural. It was ruthlessness and careless greed that was unnatural. That was what he hated.

He could hardly bear to think of the night. Yet there was so much excitement in the thought of it that he felt his heart pound and his skin prickle. There was not a thing in the world he could do to stop it. Suddenly, more than anything, he found himself not wanting to show himself either a child or a fool in the man's cool contemptuous eyes.

He must go back. The angle of the yellowing sun came from the west. His paddle slipped easily into the water, pushed, among its own swirling eddies, lifted, and dropped, pushed again with gentle motions of his arms and wrists. It was as if, even while he had been brooding, his clumsiness had changed into a good imitation of Dillon's effortless stroke. It felt right. The boat slipped along the thread of open water without a sound.

So he came to the last part of that moment in his life that he would never forget. A movement at the near bank caught his eye. He held his paddle still, and his breath.

A brown deer had stepped down among the yellowing grasses and had lowered her graceful head to drink. When she looked up he could see her black nose dripping, her big eyes brown, gleaming with watchfulness, her big furry ears twitching, the clean delicate legs. Nothing about him alarmed her although her head stayed up. Then he saw, pushing past her flanks, a spotted fawn. It was so small and delicate it seemed to him it must just have been born. Its little black hooves were tiny, its little legs like shapely sticks. It thrust its nose uncertainly into the water and snuffled and drank while its mother waited. Then another fawn moved at her other side. When the fawns' heads lifted the mother briefly drank. Her tail was twitching. She looked once or twice at the rigid boy in the boat. But she was not frightened.

Perhaps she had never been frightened by a man, he thought. Perhaps now the little spotted fawns could grow up here in peace. He had never known anything so gentle. It seemed to him he could have sat there without moving, for hours, just watching. Then they moved away.

He went back to the camp island as if he were still in a kind of dream. Dillon crouched among the bushes, peering out for him. His face was dark.

"Get in here," he said harshly. "What you been doin'? The patrol plane's due to come over anytime. Get behind the stern there and push."

They got the heavy boat up the bank among the bushes. Dillon cut some branches to cover it completely. Henry followed him silently into the deep shadow of the trees. Dillon had been cleaning his rifle. The rubber nipple was in place. Boxes of ammunition were laid out, a box of salt. He picked up the whetstone again and went on sharpening his knife.

Not knowing what else to do, Henry had a half cup of water and lay down on his blanket on the platform where Dillon sat. Above the thick canopy of leaves, the bits of sky were yellow. Then far away, he heard the little rumor of a plane's engine, high up. He would have liked to have dashed out and watched it. Suppose he ran and waved the blanket, what would happen? Nothing, he thought, even if he was seen—nothing except that Dillon would half kill him.

Dillon did not lift his head from his whetstone as the sound of the engine came over, came lower, as if to look at something below, quite near. Then it lifted and trailed its racket over the trees and was gone.

"Is it—looking for something?" Henry whispered.

"Snoopin'," Dillon said carelessly. "Lookin' to stop people doin' what they always done. Lookin' for people fishin' from boats they don't know where they are. Lookin' for stop nets on the rivers. Countin' deer. Watchin' birds. Might's well be policemen."

"You hate 'em," Henry said boldly, rolling over and staring at Dillon's hard back.

"Why not?" he said.

Twilight was drifting like green smoke under the trees. Beyond the opening of the path from the water a glimpse of the flat world beyond was a brilliant green, like glass.

Dillon moved here and there. He was fussing with a lantern. Henry lay with his hand over his eyes. He was suddenly a little frightened. He was hungry, too, but he did not want to ask Dillon if they were going to eat before. . . .

Dillon had a drink out of a bottle and stood up. "Let's get the boat back in the water while there's light," he said. Outside, the greenness was still visible and the high thin sky, where birds were moving in a long wavering ribbon, was still luminous. They shoved the boat into the water. When the ripples were still, they stood and listened. Frogs croaked and boomed nearby. There were insects in the long grass. Mosquitoes began suddenly to shrill by Henry's ear and pricked him as he slapped and stamped. He saw Dillon's head tall against the pale green sky where a star began to glitter like tinsel.

"Hark," Dillon said, with that edge to his voice that kept Henry rigid. From not very far away he heard a strange breathy roaring or booming, a great echo of sound that seemed to spread over the flat watery country like an ancient awful voice from the mud. From far away, the roaring came back. The night was full of it. It was a sound that seemed as if it had echoed here long, long before man had ever heard it—an old, old voice, the hoarse harsh echo of endless and unknown time.

The skin of Henry's neck prickled with more than mosquitoes. "What is it?" he whispered. A little whispering voice high up in the tree branches, a little throbbing sound, seemed to echo his heartbeats. He knew later on it was only an owl. Now it scared him a little.

"There they are then, those babies. Waiting for us," Dillon said cheerfully. "You never heard 'gators roarin' before, Henry? My, you got a lot to learn. Let 'em roar all they want to now. You better open you a can of beans. See 'f they's another sandwich. It's all I want. Can't risk making a fire. Might's well wait until the moon's up. Then we'll go get us some 'gators."

A Pond Full of 'Gators

THE piece of a moon that glared in the eastern sky, and glared over the Everglades, made silver of a waterway between black banks where Dillon poled his boat. Henry crouched in the bow. It was as if for the first time, staring around him, he learned what night could be like. It was like an enormous, airy, black and silver dream.

The water swished a little against the pushing bow. Dillon stood tall against the sky full of soft light. He poled so surely and so steadily that the boat never halted or went faster for a push. The rhythm of the dripping pole was the chief movement of the night.

The world was so amazing that Henry had forgotten

his dread. He was carried forward from moment to moment in which he could not look or feel or breathe deep enough. What was to come was no longer his concern.

They went much the same way they had come but he made no attempt to recognize it. Trees went over, only clotted shadows. Open banks went by. The water widened or it narrowed and night-waking creatures—herons, a rat on a bank, things he could not imagine that scuffled or slid—went by with the rest. Moon-silver softened everything.

The moon was higher when he saw trees and then the water widening by tall grasses. Dillon laid his pole in the boat and sat and handled his rifle. Henry had the lantern. That was all he had to do, turn on the light.

When Dillon was ready, he said, "OK, Henry. The light. Over there."

The beam that shot out from the lantern in his hand was a power that divided everything into darkness and dazzling light. Insects flashed white, criss-crossing it from darkness to darkness. Beetles like spots of gold rushed up the beam to the glass. Midges were a silvery cloud. Nearby sedges sprang into it. On the far bank a bush stood and glittered. Water was a swaying gray mist. Shadows were sharp. And everywhere, reflecting the powerful beam, there were dots and spots and streaks, small speckles and dashes of brightness, that were eyes. Spiders' eyes. Frogs' eyes. Lizards' eyes. Eyes of unknown and unguessed night-loving insects. The eyes of a night heron, flapping away. The eyes of turtles on the bank. Perhaps the flat-disked eyes of a wildcat, far over.

Then low, glowing, full in the light, swam two low moons, clear red—swam and drew near, were drawn by that dazzling power of the irresistible lantern. Dillon made the squeaky grunt, half throat, half stomach, that young 'gators cannot resist. Henry held the light steady, paralyzed.

He could see the shadow of the 'gator's head beyond the bumps and the eyeplates' red light. The shadowy tail moved gently, moving him forward, hypnotized, the pointed fingers of the fat front claws hanging idly. He saw the foolish, fascinated 'gator grin.

In that one moment, he thought what it must be like. He could not bear it. He switched off the light.

"You, Henry," Dillon's voice had a whiplash in it. "Put that light on. You crazy?"

The glare picked up the 'gator as it turned away. The head came around again. The body was again drawn help-lessly nearer. It wasn't fair, Henry thought wildly. His stomach pumped in protest. But he held the light.

The sound of the rifle was only a kind of plop, si-lenced by that nipple so that it could not have carried one hundred feet. The 'gator's head vanished in foam. For a minute the tail and arms thrashed. Then they were quiet and the lighter belly came up and hung. A redness like smoke spread in the lighted water.

"Right under the eye," Dillon said. "Blows off the top of the head. Only place a bullet can get through the hide."

He picked up the slender iron rod and caught the open jaw, hauling it up by the boat. "Three foot and a half," he said, pleased, and dumped it, a heavy dead thing, into the boat.

Henry looked away from it. The light was wobbling in his hand. "Steady," Dillon hissed. "Over there." Two pairs of small red moons came swimming gently into the whiteness. Very soon, Dillon lifted the slender rifle that made its flap of sound. He shot again. There was the same moment of floundering in the water, soon quiet. The boat moved easily toward the floating things. Dillon dropped them into the boat.

Henry's hands were cold on the light. All his muscles were cold and his tight jaw ached. He told himself it was exciting. It was what men did. But he could not make himself believe it was much fun. If he dropped the light in the water, they would not die. But Dillon would half kill him. He was perfectly sure of that.

The boat floated behind the broad white cone of glare. Dillon told him to sweep the width of the pond. Insects crisscrossed it wildly, midges in a silvery cloud, golden beetles that dashed up it head on, from which Henry flinched. Frogs' eyes glowed gold. Fish waked and circled hazily among the lighted lily pads. The silent wings of an owl flashed white. Strange menacing shapes on the far shore came to life in brilliance and vanished as darkness rushed back. The night walled them in. Eyes gleamed everywhere. High overhead the bright piece of a moon was dimmed.

Dillon was adjusting another rubber nipple as a silencer on the end of his rifle barrel, shot once idly to make a proper hole in it, and waited. Henry had taken his eyes away from the water to watch him. When he looked back, the light jumped in his hand and he yelled in fright.

"Keep still," Dillon hissed. "What the—" He was staring.

Low down in the lighted water two huge moons glared at them and grew larger. They were a foot apart. Henry saw a huge rounded snout sliding at them, half underwater. From the high nostrils two long silver ripples of water went away. The great body behind was a black and swollen shadow, from which the fat arms hung down. The black ridged tail behind was an easy oar, bringing the whole bloated shape nearer in the relentless light. The curves of the long mouth were stitched with teeth. Opened, and brought down over the gunwale, the power was there to smash the side of the boat to splinters. This was what an alligator could be.

Henry lifted his voice in terror, "What'll I do? He's coming."

"Put out the light then." Darkness, blindness was grateful. But the thing was there. Henry heard the little ripples made by the turning tail. Dillon's voice was quiet. "He's too big. His hide's no good." The boat slid away with the push of his paddle. "He won't let us alone now. Well, I guess that's about the crop. When I think what we'd have got in the old days. . . ."

The darkness was lighter to Henry's staring eyes as they moved down the moonlit watercourse. He straightened his crouching back, his cramped, sweating fingers. Behind them they heard the great 'gator's hollow, muddy roar going booming out into the night again, and far away, a faint answering bellow. It was over for Henry. He could breathe better. His thoughts turned from what he had done. Now he was sick for sleep.

Rolled up to his ears and his bristling hair in the cotton blanket against the stabbing mosquitoes on the platform, Henry fell headfirst down into sleep.

He woke only groggily once in the night, to a scratching and thumping among their boxes and a paper bag. Dillon clapped his hands and shouted. After a minute the scratching went on. Dillon got up, cursing, to grope at the edge of the platform. Henry saw the light flare, heard the muted whack of the rifle. Something kicked for a while among the fallen leaves. Henry was deeply asleep again before it was still.

Breakfast was only bananas and bread and a drink of water, Dillon told him, when the boy got up and stumbled down the shadowy path to the water, glittering with sunlight. "It's a shame to throw away these small 'gator tails but I can't light a fire here. No telling where the plane is this morning." Henry stood staring at him, leaning over the water from the stern of the boat. Dillon held a dead 'gator and with his knife neatly slit the hide around the lower jaw and down along the belly, where the first buttons were, to the tail. The lighter skin peeled away from the flesh like a banana skin. He sloshed the whole thing in the stained water and tossed the body away.

"Hand me that salt box," he said. When he was through with that hide it was a neat, heavily salted roll, tied with string. "It'll keep for months," he said. "But I aim to get to Tampa before then."

Henry walked away as the man reached for another 'gator. Killing things was just one way of making a living, to Dillon. The things were here for the taking. You'd be a fool not to. It meant nothing to Dillon that it was against the law. He had been here long before the law came. You had to be smarter, that was all. What Dillon could not stand, Henry saw, was to be interfered with in this country that he and men like him knew better than anybody else in the world.

Henry sat and ate, thoughtfully. It was hard to know what to think when you were a boy, smallish and fearful. There was something in him like Dillon. He hated to be chased and yelled at and told what to do. He saw how it helped to be a man like Dillon with quick hands that could do anything, and a lithe hard body gaining him ease in this difficult world. He did not hate him so much as he had because he understood him better. But he'd got no business to go around killing alligators that did not belong to him, like George, Henry thought, especially with lights and with guns that never gave them a chance. It wasn't fair. If he'd put up a fight with that biggest 'gator now—Henry grinned at himself. He was mighty glad he hadn't. But at least there'd have been some excitement in it.

Dillon came up the path with the rolled alligator hides. He fumbled among his things and brought out a bottle and sat on the platform and took a long drink. Henry watched him. "Shot a 'coon around here last night. Just skinned it. Not much money in 'coons' skins right now and this was a female, not much good. Take some more salt and rub it down good, will you? I used up the other box. I'm goin' to get some sleep."

Henry found the brindled fur in the boat, rubbed it in the salt, rolled it up and tied it, washed his hands. It was hardly an animal anymore. Out in the water garfish were pulling savagely at the skinned flesh. He sat and watched them, watched a kingfisher daring, watched the white puffs of wind clouds in the morning sky. The sun soaked into him, and the quiet. He saw how brown his hands were, harder. It seemed to him he was older than he had been—how long ago was it? It was not just that he had seen so much and learned so much as that he had lived more deeply. He had never thought so hard or so much in his whole life, or about so many things. Yet it was not queer to be sitting here and know he was somehow stronger. It felt good.

He got up and walked back among the trees. There was so much, though, that he needed to see and know. Even here. Dillon slept as quietly as an animal. Henry moved across toward the sunshine on the other side. He turned back and picked up Dillon's well-whetted machete, the knife that was as broad and long as a sword. The handle felt fine in his hand. The long blade was balanced. He took some cuts with it at the bushes. The stems fell cleanly. It was a good weapon to have.

The long dark tail of a moccasin went away at an angle from the way he was going. He saw what Dillon meant, that you had to watch out and be careful. But he did not see why he should kill it. There was swamp beyond the bushes, beyond the tall tawny grass. He moved quietly in his soft old sneakers. It looked as if there were trails through the saw grass. Perhaps deer had made them. The hope of seeing them again thrilled him. It would be wonderful to come up on them and not frighten them. It would be enough for him just to stand and watch them and not have them know he was there. Just to see how they moved, so gracefully in their freedom. He wanted to see the fawns playing together and jumping. He thought how much he would like to know all sorts of things about them—what they ate and how the little ones were born, even how the long muscles worked their delicate legs and why they jerked their pointed tails. Everything.

He stood among tufts of grass and peered here and there. There was mud at the grassroots and he had to step carefully. He saw nothing except buzzards lifting in the sky and one small impudent bright yellow bird with a black mask, like a bandit, that fussed and darted about in a bush. Once, not far away, he heard a little crash as if something had taken a quick leap among dried leaves, and he stayed still. There was nothing else. He listened. Then he moved back to where, over the grass clumps, some of which were as high as his head, he could see the top of the trees of the camp. It was windlessly hot among the grasses and sweat prickled on his skin and midges bit him.

Once he stopped, sure he heard something behind him. His heart beat a little harder but he told himself, clutching the machete handle, there was nothing to be afraid of. He turned but he heard it again. It was a queer little whimpering cry, low down. Something was moving through a patch of short wire grass. Something was whimpering and following him.

A little furry triangular face with bright eyes in a black mask like the little bird's looked up at him from the parted grasses. It went on whimpering. He was sure if he took a step toward it, it would disappear. It struggled out of the grass clump and staggered toward him. It was a baby raccoon, like a kitten. He thought he had never seen anything so neat and cute with its little furry sides, its funny, little, banded tail. He stooped and held out his hand to it and it cried and ran between his fingers. It was warm and furry. Its moist tongue licked his fingers.

It trembled as he lifted it up in both his hands, staring into its funny, eager, peak-nosed face. He couldn't help it, he cuddled it in his neck and felt on his cheek its moist nose touching and touching, not smelling, but feeling, as in his fingers he felt the pads of its delicate hands feeling, touching. It gave him a sensation that stirred him to his heart.

He took it back with him, trembling with life, with excitement, with hunger, in the crook of his arm covered with his shielding hand. When he stumbled under the trees he saw that Dillon was sitting on the edge of the platform, working at something. He was not drinking. Henry showed him, wordless with pleasure, the little raccoon in his arms.

Dillon hardly glanced at it. "Come on," he said. "Let's get going. There's no use hanging around here."

Henry said, "What can I feed him?"

"He'll eat anything. Don't give him no food of mine. I feed you. Feed him what you've got. I seen too many raccoons. Come on."

Henry managed to snatch a piece of banana while they were carrying things to the boat. The fine little black hands grasped it, the neat baby teeth worked at it avidly. It had been starving, and no wonder. Henry put it inside his shirt with a piece of bread. The crumbs tickled him as he went down to the boat, carrying some of the stuff. He felt it there, throbbing. The secret delight left him grinning.

The boat was pushed off and poled down the waterway. Dillon stood. The pole swayed back and forth. Henry sat half dreaming, hunched over the little weight in his shirtfront. It was sleeping, the little wild thing—the little thing. He had no words for the tenderness that filled him, for its smallness, its trust.

The afternoon went by him like the streaming banks, grass, trees, the narrowing or widening water. He knew it so well now. Its monotony left him free to brood, to be secret, over the new thing in his breast. He saw the ruined rookery where few cranes flew. He saw the eagle tree. The eagle, high overhead, was soaring. He did not even wonder at the man who poled and poled, with a rhythm that never faltered. Sometimes, where the water was deep in that wandering skein of watercourses, he sat and paddled.

Late in the afternoon they moved along a bank screened only by a few bushes. Beyond, grasses grew short in a kind of meadow. It was a little strange to see high firm ground after all the mud, the mangrove arches, the endless tall water-rooted grasses.

Dillon trailed his paddle. Ripples talked by the bow as the boat slowed along the shore. Dillon stood studying the grassy bank where it had been trampled to the water's edge. "Deer," he said aloud.

It was the first word Henry had heard spoken, it seemed to him, for so long that it startled him. They were well past before he recognized the word.

The little thing in his shirt had had a good sleep. Now it was stirring. Its name is Brownie, he thought. That pleased him. He had a baby raccoon and its name was Brownie.

It was extraordinary to him when he saw, on a low-dipping branch of a mangrove, a long black rag. The water was deep. They moved in a tunnel among mangroves. At the paddle, Dillon chuckled suddenly.

"Nobody's been here. Know how you can tell? See those spider's webs?"

Henry was already trying to wipe from his face the sticky strands that stretched from tree to tree across the narrow water.

"If anybody had been up here since last night, the webs would be broken. There she is." He saw nothing but mangroves.

Nothing ever tasted better to Henry than the hot supper Dillon cooked on his kerosene stove, that they ate snug in the cockpit in the cane of the leaves. The baby raccoon made funny little growls of delight in its throat as he sucked at bread dipped in condensed milk, clinging with one tiny hand to Henry's thumb. It wrinkled its long nose up at Henry, white with milk spots up to its bright beads of eyes. Then it went to sleep curled up on his shoulder under his ear. It was wonderful to stretch out sleepily on the cockpit floor after he'd washed the things, not hungry anymore.

But he woke in the night, startled, remembering what he had only vaguely heard Dillon say before he went to sleep. "Got to get goin' at first light." He was sure now that Dillon had said, "Might's well get me that deer."

134

The Labyrinth

THE faintest beginnings of light showed in the sky,
between the night-shadowed walls of trees as the
fishboat moved down the varying path of pale water.
Henry had wakened abruptly to Dillon's footsteps on
the cabin roof as he cast off the lines from the trees. His
pole bumped hollowly as he pushed the bow from the
mud. They went backward a while where the narrow
dead end of waterway opened out. He took his time
getting the bow around. Henry fended off the bumping
dinghy. When the engine roared they groped off at half
speed for a few miles as the shadows grew more dim and
the air freshened with dawn.

After that, Dillon rowed the dinghy with a towline on

the bigger boat. All Henry knew was that they were on water among mangroves. Presently there was a brightness that must have been east. Wisps of white mist wavered up from the water. White birds flew, appeared, disappeared in it. There were times when Dillon's figure, bending to his oars ahead, was only a dim shadow. The thin fog was dank. The little raccoon lay warm against Henry's skin under his shirt. It kept him from thinking too much about what Dillon was doing.

The man was keeping quiet, that was clear, finding deeper water for the fishboat, stopping off to turn and stare ahead of him. The mangroves covered them to the right of the stream as they moved cautiously. The other bank, as the mist thinned, opened out among grasses. Beyond there Henry recognized with surprise the eagle tree, and the eagle hunched squarely on a branch, staring at the light coming up the sky.

The boat stopped moving under the arching trees. Dillon brought up the dinghy silently, hand over hand on the wet towline. He eased the dinghy alongside, stepped into the cockpit and fastened it before he ducked into the cabin. When he came out, he had his rifle.

He never looked at Henry but motioned him from the stern seat and crouched there, looking at an angle over at the other bank. The mist was empty by the water's edge. Henry stood near. His heart was beating so hard he thought the man would have heard it. He was cold and shaking with rage and fright and a kind of sickness. If the deer came, he could not think of anything he could do.

The deer was there. He could tell by the muscles tensing in the man's back, the rigidity of his neck. He could see only a shadow behind a clump of bushes. Light was more golden on the thinning mist. The deer was golden brown in a streak of light. Henry saw a round ear twitching. Dillon was lifting his gun.

The sound of a hoof clicking on a rock came distantly across the water's stillness. The deer stood, stepped toward the water, snuffed down at it, was lifting its head.

Dillon cuddled the gun butt in his shoulder, tensed his elbow—Henry yelled. He beat down on the man's shoulder and screamed, high and dreadfully. He was frightened to death but he could not stop. Dillon put down his gun and got up and turned to look down at him, his face a cold, yellowish, savage mask. The deer had vanished.

Dillon hissed, "Stop it—shut up—you gone crazy? I swear I'll kill you."

Henry stopped yelling, backing away before the deadly hard hands coming at him to strike.

"Don't you touch me," he croaked, backing. The man followed him, step by step, deliberately cornering him. The glint in his narrow eyes, the twist on his thin lips, was pure hate. Henry shrieked in despair, "You killed my 'gator! You kill everything! Don't you touch me, you killer—"

The man had him just where he wanted him, in the angle of the deckhouse. His weight came forward with his strike. Henry went down, a kind of helpless dive forward between the man's legs, scrambling with all his weight. The man made one startled sound, then he fell forward. His head hit. He was lying down on the deck, in the corner.

Henry waited, breathing hard, shivering from head to foot. Dillon did not move. Henry looked at the arm and hand that were stretched out on the deck. The fingers uncurled and went limp and heavy. The arm was motionless. He could not see the man's face. It was hidden by his shoulder, which was jammed into the corner at a queer angle. The shoulder did not move.

Henry straightened up, watching him like a cat. Maybe Dillon was only making believe, lying there waiting for him to stoop over and take a closer look, waiting to grab his ankle or his arm with that quiet, steely hand. But it was still.

"Dillon," he whispered once. There was no answer. He cleared his throat and spoke louder. "Dillon!"

A crow flew over, cawing. Leaves brushed the top of the wooden awning as the breeze blew. There was no other sound.

Henry stepped watchfully nearer. He prodded the bottom of Dillon's foot with a careful toe. "Dillon," he shouted and bent over, trying to see his face. His eye was shut and his cheek was a queer yellowish white, like the underside of a turtle.

The stillness, giving back his shout, frightened him. Henry turned and looked all around. The first brightness of the sun touched the bare top of the eagle tree.

As he stared upward, locked and stiff in a new kind of dread, the eagle lifted, flapped, rose up, and soared, and all his head was gold.

It was an accident, Henry thought wildly. He had not meant to do anything but save the deer. He had not thought at all that Dillon would rage so. He was only defending himself, only keeping the man from hurting him. He had a right to do that.

But now the man lay quiet there on the floor boards and Henry thought, "He's dead. I've killed him." He could not go any nearer. He could not bear to touch him. All he wanted was to think and keep away.

The baby raccoon on his shoulder was nibbling his ear and whimpering with hunger. He was hungry himself, starved. He went below and lighted the kerosene stove and cooked bacon and fried eggs. He fixed the raccoon some condensed milk and bread and fed him the bacon rind. He made himself some coffee.

But his hands jerked so that he spilled half the coffee on the floor. He was eating standing up, cramming food into his mouth and breathing hard at the same time, and coughing. He could not turn his back on the ladder or take his eyes away from that one foot of Dillon's that he could see, bottom up on the deck, at a level with his gaze. It had not moved once.

Henry ate faster and faster, nearly choking himself with a hasty swallow of coffee. It was growing more and more plain to him that he could not stay here in the boat any longer. He had to get away—anywhere—and fast. He had no idea what could happen now but he could not stay to see it.

He tried to put his mind to thinking what he would need, picking things up and putting them down. He nearly tripped and fell over the little raccoon that growled at him in fright as he stumbled. He picked it up and cuddled it in his neck. "Keep still," he said. "Somebody will hear you." And his own voice brought out the chill gooseflesh on his back and made him start up the ladder and peer about. There was no one anywhere but Dillon, who somehow now began to look no more than a heap of shirt and old pants.

Henry began to think slowly and carefully. He must take what he needed and get out and go. He took the machete and a fishing rod and a blanket and put it in the dinghy. He lifted over one of the heavy demijohns of water. He thought of matches and a sack of canned things, including milk, and his knife. He looked at the rifle and let it lie. Then he picked up his raccoon, stepped over the gunwale and into the dinghy, untied it, headed its bow around, and paddled in the direction from which they had come.

What he had to be careful about, he was thinking, was not getting back to the right into that watercourse that, a mile or two afterward, led to the dead end among the mangroves. He tried to keep to the deeper water to the left, hoping that presently he would feel some little pull of a current moving as if, far away south and west, a slow tide worked its way out to open seawater.

What was left of that ruined rookery went by him, hardly noticed. The crows were gone. The stick nests were dried and dropping. His eye followed the lines of a moccasin sunning on the mud. It did not matter now. The boat moved with slow thrusts of his paddle, rustling sometimes among low dropping leaves. The little raccoon was asleep beside him on the seat, curled up in a furry ball, its head upside down, ears pressed flat on the warm wood. The day was gold and gray around him, blue over the streak of the brown water. The boat and he in it moved as if he were in a dream in which he thought nothing, felt nothing, except that he was free.

The whole day went like that, among the endless green of leaves, the steady feeling of the boat under him. Where he moved now there were few grassy banks and little sunny openness. The arches of the mangroves stretched away in shadow. When he moved beyond one tree, leaning out in the water, there were trees exactly like it going away ahead.

Sometimes he found himself in a place where the trees shut down on the water and no stream led beyond. Then he saw he had taken the wrong turning and went back to the wider place and tried to see which way the deeper water went, and follow it. The sun was high overhead and he rummaged among the cans, opened one with the knife and ate—it hardly mattered what. It all tasted good. He fed the little raccoon and played with it until they both fell asleep in the bottom of the boat and the boat drifted or stopped. He did not care.

It was wonderful to be alone and here. He waked and lay staring upward into white clouds. Where the sun was located now must be the west, he thought. He ought to be trying harder to go there, and for an hour he paddled steadily. When he stopped, the trees and the opening or narrowing shapes of the brown water seemed exactly the same.

By evening he tied the boat to a great leaning trunk of a tree. He sat for a while staring down into the brown water at the soft mud of the bottom, which was filled with decaying leaves. There were some very small fish in there and some crablike things, crawling about aimlessly. He watched a big spider with long front legs on a branch above, launching a shining fine cable of web out across the water on the little wind. The spider seemed to spin it out endlessly. He could see it blowing out longer. He saw the surface of the water turn dusty in a streak of sun, and watched bugs that he remembered someone had called "water skaters" slide about on it. When he looked up again, the spider's cable had caught to some leaf across there and held. The spider was running across, trailing another strand. The tough fine line jerked with the spider's busyness.

The boy's eyes blinked. He and the raccoon had their suppers half asleep. He wondered why he was so sleepy. The blanket felt good even if the boards below his bony small shoulders and hips were increasingly hard.

But in the night once he jerked awake and sat up, cold with fright. An echo of a long scream came to him from just across the water. It sounded like his own scream back there. He did not want to think of that. It was black and strange to be sleeping there, alone. He heard the long hooting of owls. Something moved and crackled among branches beyond the bow. Something heavy thumped into the very boat.

His baby raccoon set up a baby kind of barking. It did not seem frightened. Against a shine of starlight in the water he saw a hunched shape. A big raccoon. He banged with his machete on the boards and it climbed out and went away. He remembered Dillon had said these mangroves were alive with raccoons that came down to pick at the 'coon oysters on the arched roots. They must live there, Dillon had said, in spite of the water's being too brackish to drink. Henry stuck a finger overboard and tasted it. Yes, it was brackish. The raccoons must be able to live in these treetops a long time without freshwater unless they lapped at the dew-wet leaves, or leaves that for a little while held rain. Dillon had taught Henry so much. Everything that he did here copied him or remembered him or imitated him. But he was dead.

Henry slept again, attaching no emotion now to that memory, except that he did not hate him anymore. When he woke, just after sunrise the next morning, rain was falling in gray sheets and he and his cotton blanket were soaked through and he was shivering. His body ached from the hard boards and he wished he had some hot coffee. The bread was a soggy mass in its paper bag and even the raccoon seemed to want something else. What he had was a can of stewed tomatoes with bread in it. He looked soberly at the rest of his cans in the sack. There were only six left. He'd have to get out of here.

He paddled hard for at least two hours with the same rain falling, pitting endlessly the tin-colored water, rattling on the rubbery green leaves. He saw no birds— nothing but a few ducks hugging on the banks. He found what he was sure was a current moving out.

He was warmed by the paddling. The sun came out for a little while. Before the rain began again, he found he was paddling straight into a mangrove island, under whose tall columns and interwoven roots the water disappeared. He had taken some wrong turning again. It rained as he went back. The gray clouds moved at the top of the trees. Some white birds stood still, hunched up in the wet, in a low swampy place. They rose up before him and swerved away in silence. When it was not raining, the leaves and his paddle dripped.

The wide water he followed narrowed again. He hunted here and there among the branches for an outlet. There was none. Now in the rain he could not tell which way was west. What he must keep to and follow carefully, he thought, was the wide deep water. He had let himself go mooning along without paying enough attention. It was stupid of him. He knew just what Dillon would have said.

By nightfall, with an inch of water sloshing in the boat and water running down his chilled skin from his soaked shirt and shorts, he was tied up under another mangrove, only a little taller and darker overhead than the first. His arms ached with paddling. The boat must have traveled miles and miles. But in the rain, with the sky obscured, he had no way of telling where he was going. By morning, with the sun out . . .

The night was a misery of wetness and coldness and hardness. Sometimes it rained again. But more often he had to pull the wet blanket over his head to keep from being stung to death by a horde of screaming mosquitoes. He began to think he had been foolish to leave the fishboat. At least the cabin was warm and dry. He dozed, thinking that Dillon was there, cooking something hot, sneering at him for running away. When he woke, it was hard for him to remember that Dillon was dead.

There was sun that morning burning beyond the white veil of the river mists, warming the light and the rising birds. He started paddling before he had anything to eat. The boat's nose shoved slowly through the mists. He could see only the nearest leaves. But the mist was thinner. Up ahead, above mist, he saw a whole treeful of black water turkeys, sitting motionless, spreading out their wings stiffly to dry, turning their sharp heads on their long snaky necks to watch him. Dillon had said they did that because they had no oil on their wings to help them dive underwater for fish. So they had to be always drying their soaked feathers after they had their breakfasts.

He found a good wide channel and paddled it briskly until he glanced up and saw the sun over the treetops. It was in the wrong place, he was going northeast. It was too bad to have lost an hour's work but he couldn't help it. He waited and ate something and turned back. This was better. He was drying in the sun. Birds were soaring. There was even, he began to think, a little current swirling ahead. He followed it. But the trouble was, the water branched into two or three currents. He threw twigs and watched them move. It seemed to him the left one was fastest. But he meant to remember, from this place, there was a middle one and a left-hand one, all going away among identical mangrove branches.

The left-hand current branched and branched again. It narrowed. There was nothing ahead but leaves. He must go back. He was hot now. He tried to get back to the place from which the currents had seemed to branch. He never saw it again. Everywhere now, it seemed to him, there was nothing but those heavy leaves. They reached out for him, blocked his way and covered up with their shadowy branches the flow of water.

He stopped paddling. There was no need to hold on to anything. He was lost, and he knew it. There was no way he could think of that he could ever get out again.

He sat still in the boat, hunched over with his head in his hands, in dismay and exhaustion. The baby raccoon climbed into the crook of his arms and cuddled there. His hand, where blisters had broken and were stinging, smoothed the brindled fur.

There was one way, he remembered suddenly. If he could find an open bit of ground and build a fire the rangers, perhaps the plane, as well as the powerful boats, could find him. But if so, what would they do to him for killing Dillon? No—the thought was so terrible that he picked up the paddle again.

The boat had drifted. So there must be some kind of current, somewhere. It lead straight ahead under deep boughs. When he pushed in he saw a little brown trace of water in shadow. The bottom scraped once. He could only pole. The boat went forward in a kind of brown gloom. When he stopped pushing, all around him the great mangrove forest thrust straight upward from the arched roots, tall shafts under the roof of leaves. In there, it seemed to him, no birds moved or called, there were no fish in the shallow waters, there was nothing but silence.

He could not go back. He had to push forward. It was hot and there were midges. Ahead, he thought it was brighter. The trees opened out a little. The water was deeper. But there were the leaves again, hemming him in. It was as if the flow of the water ended here. He sat again as he had before. Now he was really lost. The silence was deep here as it had been in the hollow shades of the forest. Or what was that sound? It was the loud buzzing of an insect. Or another sound, very far away. It reminded him a little of the drone of an outboard motor. Far to the right. Sometimes it stopped. Sometimes it went on. It *was* an outboard motor.

He shouted once. He was too excited. The leaves swallowed up his voice. It was over there. He pushed at the pole. The boat went in among the leaves and stopped. When he cleared them away before his eyes and mouth the same arches were there, but beyond there was sunlight on what could only be open ground.

His hands trembled so he could hardly hold the machete. He put matches in his shirtfront and the raccoon baby on his shoulder. He was so stiff from sitting that his knees creaked as he tried to climb along a branch, holding on to another. Once his foot slipped and one foot went down into sucking mud. He hauled himself up and went on with difficulty but with quivering caution.

There was a tuft of grass to step on. He got down off the last branch and walked on weedy sandy earth. Sun was hot on him.

When he listened he could not hear the outboard anymore. He was going straight across anyhow. There must be deeper water beyond there. He pushed among vines and jungle trees and more open ground.

On the other side, back to him, staring up at a tree, in brown khaki pants and a long shirt, with a khaki cap over his ears was the queerest looking boy. He could almost not believe it. But he shouted hoarsely and stumbled as the figure turned. It wasn't a boy. It was a little old woman. Her bobbed white hair stuck out under her cap all around her pleasant face. Her calm eyes were bright, bright blue.

"Well for pity's sake," she said. "What on earth happened to you?"

To Lostman's

HE realized suddenly how wild he must look—scratched, burned, his shirt in rags, his uncombed sun-bleached hair matted with leaves, and all filthy. It was all he could do, for a minute, to keep from crying because she was a kind woman.

"I—got lost," he said. "I couldn't get my boat out."

"Alone? Where'd you come from?" Her face was more and more astonished.

He gestured vaguely. "But all in there's the Labyrinth," she said. "Anybody that gets in there could stay lost a long time. It goes on all the way in back of these rivers, nothing but mangroves and ponds of brackish water. I wouldn't risk it for anything. Are you hungry?"

"Not much," he said. "I had some stuff. I just want to—get out."

"I don't really see how anybody ever let you get in. Wasn't anybody with you? What were you doing?"

"A man—got hurt," he said vaguely. "I was going to get somebody . . ." It had not occurred to him before that he must have some kind of story to tell. It had begun to seem to him he might die in there and never see anybody again. "Can't I get my boat out?"

She said, "Where is it?" When he pointed she shook her head. "I wouldn't dare to try. First thing, we'd both be lost. I know where I am now but that's only because I'm always awfully careful. Where the chart doesn't show the way, I tie a rag on a bush. I'm about ready to go back now. You feel all right? Where'd you get the cute little raccoon? You could help me put out the last of these snails."

He stared at the open box she had in her hand. It was full of what looked like big, thin, colored buttons or like bubbles—pale yellow and cream color, pale pink or rosy, streaked with fine black lines. "Liguus," she said. "Didn't you ever see any tree snails before?"

"Are they alive?" he said. She put one in his grimy hand, a pointed pale yellow shell banded with gray, delicate as a flower. The feel of the funny sticky snail's foot, as it came out on his palm and began to flow across it, tickled and delighted him. "Lookit the way it's going. Lookit the little horns."

She liked him for his pleasure in it. "My husband

used to collect them by the thousands down here," she said briskly. "It seemed too bad to me to take them away. We kept some alive and when he died, I made up my mind to bring them back. Put that one on his tree here. It's a gumbo-limbo. You know its name?"

He shook his head, lifting the snail to the branch covered with red papery bark.

"They'll grow here," she said. "Put out some more. Not too many to a tree. I wish you could see the beauties that came from Cuba. Big as walnuts. Maybe these came from there first, thousands of years ago, drifted over on a branch in some hurricane. There. That's good. This is the last box. Where they grow in one spot sometimes they will all be the same color with new bandings, not like the rest. I figured that way up here people would let them alone to grow. It's against the park law to collect them, of course, but you know how people are. Come along now. What's your name?"

He was close behind her quick heels, going fast through the tall weeds. "Henry," he said vaguely. He had almost forgotten it.

"I'm Dr. Trotter," she said. "Everybody thinks that's funny because it's the way I walk. And my husband was Dr. Trotter, too. He was a physician and I was a baby doctor and then a botanist. I was going around looking at orchids. Not in the mangroves, of course, but up in the real jungles—hardwoods, live oaks, sweet gum, that sort of thing. Lots of native orchids, the little brown and yellow ones are charming, I always think. Oncidium—but you couldn't be expected to know that—then I got interested in the tree snails and I like to think I'm really doing some good, bringing them back up here. It's such a pleasure to keep things alive, don't you think? But of course you do. I can see you've been kind to that dear little raccoon. Wasn't it fortunate I found this good landing for the boat just under the bank here? Don't slip now. It's right here."

He would have followed that extraordinary, cheery, warm woman-chatter for miles and miles, hardly listening, knowing only that somehow he was safe. Her little boat lay below a grassy bank in water wider than any stream he had seen all day. He looked down into it with surprise and pleasure. It was exactly the right kind of boat to have, painted pale blue. It had a little cockpit and a little cabin and a mast so that she could sail it, but an outboard motor, too. It had a little dinghy like a pointed saucer made of glass. And the cozy cabin was all cluttered up with the nicest things. Besides the fish lines, there were bright cushions and pictures of birds and books full of pictures and cans of things like cookies and a little stove with something cooking on it and a little oven with something baking in it that smelled like gingerbread.

She had jumped in and whisked down into the cabin and whisked out again while he was still staring from the bank. "You hand me down the machete and your raccoon, and take this towel and soap and go right down there by the bush and give yourself a good scrubbing from head to foot. I must say I've almost never seen any-body quite so . . . then when you're dry you can put on this old shirt—let's see, and a pair of shorts—good thing I sometimes wear boys' clothes on board, isn't it? Then I thought we'd just have some hot food—run along now, Henry. I'll give the raccoon some milk."

It was wonderful to be scrubbed clean. It was wonder-ful to eat hot beef stew and hot buttered gingerbread. It was wonderful to hear the uproar of the little outboard kicking away at the foamy water behind and see the banks go moving by, fast. But most wonderful of all was to sit and see her brown fist on the tiller and watch the pleas-ant snap of her blue eyes as she took the boat confidently down the widening river—and him with it, safe. It was like coming out of a nightmare.

He listened gravely and attentively to her stream of talk that sometimes, over the racket, he could under-stand. "There's my white rag," she said pointing. "That's the last one I tied before I stopped. It would be on the right going down, see? This is right—it's too easy to get lost. Here's the place I stayed the night. There's some big trees in there and I put out at least two dozen snails. Yes, here's my next rag, we turn here. You see, none of these little streams are on the chart. There's too many of them. But people are so careless. I think you must have been unnecessarily careless, Henry. It's too bad about your boat."

He nodded and smiled at her at regular intervals. He thought she was the nicest woman he had ever known—and smart. He didn't know women could be so smart, running the boat all by herself, tying those rags on. . . .

"Aren't you ever scared of snakes?" he shouted.

She smiled at him gaily. "People always ask me that," she shouted. Her white hair blew away from her little old face with its smiling wrinkles. The trees blew away backward from them. The bright spray flew. His drying shorts flapped from a stay. The speed, the noise, the getting away, everything she said, was wonderful. "But I always tell them, I say, I never go fast enough on any of this dry land here to overtake the snakes. Sometimes I see their tails crawling away. But I make plenty of noise. Sometimes I talk to them."

Henry laughed out loud at that. He'd bet she talked to them! But she nodded and laughed with him and went on shouting, "And then they ask me how I can stand the mosquitoes. And I tell them I wear these boys' long pants and underneath I put on two pairs of silk stockings, and I mean silk, and you know, it bends their beaks—I do really think it does. And, of course, these long sleeves. There's my third rag. Good. Then we have to cross over to the left. You see, you can't always tell by the way the current seems to be going. Sometimes it's only the wind blowing it. When the tide comes in below it pushes it up in funny ways and that's very confusing."

He looked at her respectfully and nodded several times. "I know all about that," he shouted. "You can't tell a thing. It's terrible."

To his surprise, suddenly, she switched off the ignition. The boat went on for a minute, then slowed, nosing into the bushes. She was leaning forward, staring at him.

"Henry," she said. Her voice was clear in the stillness. "Henry, I've let myself forget—what was it you said, that a man was sick back there? You mean, you're going for help?"

He stared at her blankly, hunched up on the seat. There it was. Her blue glance fixed him. "There was— there was a man in a boat—he looked sick, I mean, he was lying down—and he—he'd hit his head, I guess."

"Did they send you for help?"

"There wasn't anybody else."

"You mean, you were on the boat with him when he was hurt?"

"I guess—yes, I was."

"And that's how you got lost, looking for help. But why didn't you tell me?"

"I forgot."

She was so surprised the whites of her eyes showed all around the blue. "You forgot? But how in he world . . . you mean, you'd been lost so long you lost track!"

He was nodding. That must have been it. But still her face was puckered up with that strange way of some grown people, as if they could tell that he had more in his mind than what he said.

"But Henry, what was he—"

The racket of a heavy boat engine was coming toward

them along one of those wandering rivers beyond that might, or might not, open up into this one. She turned her head and listened. Across the widening stream there was one of those islands of solid land, with only a few fringing mangroves and the sun shining on an open, scrubby sort of meadow, fairly high out of the water. Below it, from that other stream, a big boat came slowly. There were two or three men in it standing by the cabin, but there was a very strange thing humping up across the stern. It was a kind of wire cage with something big and black in it.

"Well, for mercy sake," Dr. Trotter said. "That's a black bear. That's the ranger's boat. What on earth . . . ?"

The boat slowed, headed out into the stream, reversed its engines, and backed into the high bank. A ranger, all wide hat and neat uniform, jumped out to throw a line over a tree and make it fast. The other ranger climbed on top of the cage as the black bear tried to stand up and claw his polished shoes.

Henry could hear their loud cheerful voices and their laughter. A man in the middle of the boat stood with some metal thing in his hand. The man on top of the cage slowly pulled up the sliding door. The other prodded the bear with the end of a boat hook through the bars. The big black bear stuck his head out of the door, humped up and sniffing suspiciously, as if he had stood so much that he was taking even an opening to freedom with extreme caution. Suddenly he dashed out to solid ground, stood on his haunches sniffing, and then turned suddenly, as if he could not stand it, and began to waddle back to his cage.

Henry could see his long pale nose, the great claws on his shuffling feet, the rough dark fur of his pelt. The men were laughing. The man with the metal thing raised it and it hissed and popped in the bear's face.

"It's a fire extinguisher," Dr. Trotter exclaimed. "Of all the . . . !"

The bear reared up, enormous and black, snorting, shaking his heavy head. Then he dropped and turned and shuffled off as fast as he could run, as if at last he were going home.

One smiling ranger saw the little old woman and the boy watching them in surprise and waved. The boat was being shoved out into the stream, nearer them. "Hi, Mrs. Doc," the ranger said. "How'd you like our new bear? A state game warden caught him upstate and said we could have him."

"Will he like it here?" Henry piped up.

"He'll love it. There used to be a lot of bears in the dry 'glades, big as three hundred pounds. You two doing all right?"

"Mr. Caldwell," Dr. Trotter said firmly, "I want to talk to you a minute." She turned her blue gaze on Henry and his heart sank. "You see this boy? I picked him up half starved, wandering across a dry island back there on the edge of the Labyrinth. I think he's got something to tell you. You tell him, Henry."

Henry's mouth dried up. He'd forgotten for a little while how much a ranger was like a cop. "I—well, I—"

"How'd you get here, Henry?"

"With a dinghy. I couldn't get it any farther. So I had to walk."

"But where were you?"

"Up there somewhere." He waved a vague hand.

"In somebody's boat?"

He nodded. "A man. A fisherman. He fell down and hit his head. I think he was dead."

The man had a nice face. His brown eyes were direct and kind. He had taken off his wide-brimmed hat and his hair was thin, although he didn't look old. His mouth was not severe but Henry could see authority in it. He was not a man you could lie to with any comfort.

"Did you feel if his heart was still beating?"

Henry could not say, "I wouldn't have touched him for money."

"How do you now he wasn't just knocked out?"

Henry could only shake his head.

"What was he doing up there, hunting something?"

Henry did not meet his eyes when he shook his head this time. He was not ready to talk about the alligators.

"So you came away to get help and got lost? And you haven't any idea at all where you were? Was he your father? What was his name?"

A loud squawk suddenly came from a thing by the wheel of the ranger's boat, where the other men were sitting quietly looking with interest at Henry. He could hardly tell the words that the squawks were speaking, but they all listened hard. "Squawk—squawk," the voice said. "Stop nets—got him cold—hurry—Harney River, south branch—squawk—squawk."

"That's Ralph," a man said.

Mr. Caldwell put his hat on firmly, stood to the wheel. The men were eager. Then the ranger looked back at Henry. "Get in with us, boy," he said. "We got to make time, to pick up a stop-netter. Then we'll go up to Lostman's and I can radio the plane to start searching for your father. Thanks a lot, Mrs. Doc. You did a good job with the boy."

"I'll be along to Lostman's myself by dark," she said. "So I'll see you again, Henry." She nudged him and glanced into the cabin where the baby raccoon was a furry ball of sleep.

"Thanks," he said. She meant the rangers wouldn't want him to carry a baby raccoon. She patted his shoulder as he climbed stiffly into the big boat. He hated to leave her, the little boat, the rest of the gingerbread, the coziness—besides, what would they do with him?

The ranger boat roared down the river, big, powerful, with huge engines and authority. Henry sat uncertainly on a long box and the men stood grouped under the big wooden awning behind the glass shield where the spray dashed and Mr. Caldwell, with his hat on the back of his head, stood turning the wheel. The boat sluiced around curves, rushed past echoing leafy islands, went straight by channel markings, ripped and tore and smashed through the brown water, with its wake humping up under the boat's stern. The dinghy towed with its bow always stiffly riding that wave, and the water widening out behind sloshed steadily up the muddy banks.

Henry had no idea how long it was. Once the glittering plane came over shatteringly low, and it wagged its wings and raced upward again and its squawking voice from the box said, "He's there still; he hasn't started to haul."

They laughed as they came out suddenly beyond the last mangroves into the pale wide water of the Gulf of Mexico, and the boat picked up another notch of speed and the spray flew and they bounced heavily, going fast on the slow-rolling water.

If Henry had not been so worried about everything, he would have loved it. They were far out from the green line of the shore now. The salt wind came still from the western horizon.

He was thinking, Suppose he wasn't dead and I left him to die—what will they think of that? Suppose he was dying—how many nights is it—how many days? He saw every angle of the man's strange sprawl. Suppose he wanted water and could not get to it—or food? He remembered the bread he had taken—the food he had been given freely. If he's alive still, it's not by any help from me. If he's dead, did I kill him, twice?

Man Hunt

THE rangers got up the narrowing stream just in time. They rowed quietly from the place where they cut their engine and left the big boat with one ranger in it. Ranger Caldwell let Henry go along in the dinghy. High overhead the park plane circled, a silver watchful gleam. After about a mile, they poked around a curve and there, ahead, were the nets.

They were strung on stakes right across the stretch of water from bank to bank to catch a big school of mullet and snapper as it came down with the outgoing tide. Henry could see the man sitting in his boat by the bank, watching the muddy shallows boiling and dimpling and flopping with trapped and dying fish. It would have been a great haul. The men were near enough to touch the net before the fisherman, a gray-headed stooped man, turned and saw them. His face, bitter under the unshaven bristles, went white with outrage. He stood up and made one violent gesture as if he would have torn the net apart.

But, as Mr. Caldwell spoke to him quietly, he dropped his stiff arms. He watched in silence as they loosened the nets from the posts, beginning at the bank. The milling mass of fish poured out of the opening end, silvery backs and pale bellies struggling and sliding, and flashed downstream. In a moment the mud flats were empty of fish.

The man was old and Henry was sorry for him. "Will he go to jail?" he asked the young ranger, Harry Brown— the one he liked especially.

"He'll have to stand trial. The penalty is jail and a fine. But he's so old, we'll ask the judge to let him go, but take his boat and nets. Some of these old-timers are the stubbornest of the lot. They hate us for trying to stop them doing what they've always done. He's the first stop-netter we've taken, thanks to the plane. Usually, when they hear us coming, they tear a hole in the net and let all the fish out, so there's no evidence the stream was blocked. Maybe the word will get around."

The big boat came up and they gathered in the net. A ranger got in the boat with the fisherman. They all racketed down the river together until the captured boat went south to Whitewater and Flamingo as the park boat turned north.

It was bright afternoon. The shadows of round white wind clouds lay wrinkled over the running waves of the great gulf, clear and pale to the western sky. Mr. Caldwell left the wheel to young Ranger Brown and rummaged in the icebox for soft drinks for them all and a big box of store cookies.

Things always seemed better after you ate something, Henry thought, trying to turn his mind away from thoughts of the old man's miserable face and of Arlie Dillon back there somewhere, alive or dead.

That seemed a long time ago.

It was a long slow hour as the boat rushed northward, seawater spinning by, the spray leaping as the bow came down spanking hard on the rising waves. To the east, the coast slid south, solidly banked low green. Sometimes there were islands. Sometimes there was a long beach. The men were silent.

Then ahead, high on its bank in the shade of tall trees at the mouth of Lostman's River, was the ranger station. Henry followed them up the dock steps, up the pine-needled slope to the screened house with its neat, official look.

He could sit where he liked, do what he pleased. The water spread shining below and southward. Across the river he could look at trees and a long sandbar and beach. The wind came cool in the silence. He liked everything here. But he was listening anxiously to Mr. Caldwell working the radio conversation with Homestead, asking for the plane to swing back to look for a man and a boat that were lost.

Henry had told him as well as he could where he thought the place might be. Henry thought of that endless Labyrinth, only a little part of the great mangrove country that shrouded all this end of the land, and of Dillon's dinghy he had abandoned there. How could they find anything in all that?

Soon behind him the voice from the plane squawked. It was flying out there now, low and high. Two hours went by. Once he saw a wink of metal high up. The voice squawked regularly. So far, nothing had been found.

Afternoon was going. Light was changing. Water was blue with wind. To the east, light clouds at the horizon over the dull green world were turning silvery blue. Western clouds stood dark, edged with burning light. Wind sighed in the tall leaved trees overhead.

The voice from the box reported he had seen nothing of a man and a boat. It would soon be too late to see anything. The plane went back to Homestead.

Sometimes Henry got up and wandered around on the good, dry, high ground. Sometimes he sat motionless. How many nights was it since he had left Dillon? He could not get them straight. The shadows of the dark tree would be covering the hidden boat. What was Dillon doing? Had he moved? Was he lying still as he had been when Henry left him for dead?

Behind him the house was lighted like a lantern shining out high over the twilit waters, under a sky thickening with cloud. Men's voices were cheerful, or silent. They were at ease, even if a man was lost out there, because they had done what they could. It made you feel different, Henry saw clearly.

Down there in the broad shield of water a small boat was coming up, trailing an endlessly widening wake. He heard the little beating of its engine. It headed straight for the dock.

He got up and shouted and ran down there, as if he were released suddenly from thoughts too old and heavy for a boy to bear. "It's Dr. Trotter!" he shouted. "Hi, hi, Doc Trotter—hi—"

She smiled over at him, bringing her boat up swishing in a competent turn to the empty side of the wharf. Men came down the path to help her. He was never so glad to see anyone in his life. Henry was first to catch her line, make it fast, and jump aboard to toss the stern line to a ranger's hands. When her engine was still, she asked, "Well, everybody, what happened? Did you get the stop-netter? What about Henry's man?"

She had a little light in the cabin that pulled down over a narrow little table that just fitted between the two bunks. Henry sat there with an elbow on the table and one hand fondling the baby raccoon, which chewed his fingers in his lap or climbed up his shoulder to feel his face with its funny little cushiony nose. He could see out the door to the west, which was still blue with the last light, while she stirred things on the little stove and fussed around, her hatless hair white over her pleasant face that seemed to smile with a dozen changing wrinkles. The boat joggled a little. They were half shut in and safe and at home.

She had baked potatoes that gushed out white and hot to a big piece of butter and thick hot ham slices and little hot biscuits with strawberry jam, and there were onions fried delicately brown and a big cup of cocoa for him. There was more gingerbread, after all, just as good cold as it had been hot. She sat and watched him clean up his plate twice and feed his potato skins to the little raccoon, with two cold biscuits and some canned milk. The little furry sides stuck out hard. "My stomach feels just like that, only there's no fur," he said, blinking a little drowsily.

He could say anything in the world to her that popped into his head and the calm acceptance in her blue eyes would not change. There was no comfort like it.

"You're a very satisfactory boy to cook for, Henry," she said, cleaning things up. Then she put her elbows on the table. She had on some kind of a pink thing. Her soft old cheeks were pink. She said, "Now, Henry, I think the time has come when you ought to tell me everything about yourself and this man on the boat."

Well, the time had come, all right. There was nothing else for him to do, or that he wanted to do. Some parts of it were hard to say—about his mother and about the time he left the boat and about Arlie Dillon lying there, and Henry's thinking he was dead but not really knowing. But he told it all and was glad to, tumbling it all out to her listening, responsive eyes. When it was over, he took a deep breath. He would not have been ashamed to let her see him cry. But he saw now, clearly, that crying was behind him.

She said, "Well, my goodness. What a thing. But the plane couldn't find him."

"He put the boat where it couldn't. He was always thinking about it. Anybody'd have to know just where to look. And even then . . ."

"But what can they do?"

He said slowly, "Can I see your chart?"

They spread it out, on the table. "Shark River to Lostman's River. It was all flat yellowy green for the land, marked and threaded and spotted with watercourses, blue for shallow water, white for water deep enough for boats. Looking at it, nobody could have any idea of that terrible bewilderment of brown water and dark green oily mangroves. Many parts of it had never been mapped at all. But the outlines were there.

He could follow with his finger the channel markings, east to west, of Whitewater Bay that led to the gulf. But they had turned off somewhere. "Look," he said. "There is a cutoff into the Little Shark. I remember. Then we went along there, to the place where the Shark branched off. There's a stream going south. Look, this one does— and branches. It's in there somewhere. I see now where

I got lost. I turned south into all this. Oooh! It's awful to be lost in there. Down here somewhere must be where you found me."

"Yes," she said. "I marked it in pencil. There."

"Then he's up in there," he said, marking out a wide place. He's got to be. Let's go tell them. Look, you tell them. If they'll let me go up in the plane, I can find him."

In the next hours there was a lot of talk by telephone with headquarters. The trouble was, there was no proper landing strip on the west coast, south of the town of Everglades. It was two hours there and at least four to Homestead.

The men talked in the bright room, turning from time to time and looking down gravely at Henry, who was sitting there straight, turning his eyes quickly from one face to another. It was serious, they said. The man might not be dead yet. If he had been able to move his boat out he would have been seen. He had been there for too many nights. How many? They looked at Henry. His face flushed. Four or five. Or more. Their eyes did not judge him but he was suddenly, deeply, ashamed.

There was that stretch of marl prairie, northeast, Mr. Caldwell was saying. It was dry enough there for the plane to land and take off. They could have the boy there at dawn, with the marked chart. They could not afford to lose any more time. This was a new thing to Henry—that there were men who would take all this trouble to save a man, any man.

The air was chill, the sky faintly lighted with dawn.

They stood about him, tall man-figures, silent, as men are that time before sunrise. Not Henry. No one now was so wide, staring, stark awake, tingling awake, deep-breathing, shaken-with-excitement awake. He would have overflowed with talk except that he had to see everything, hear everything, smell everything, feel everything. The chart was clutched in his hand. His knees shook. Sometimes his throat would not swallow. For the moment, he was lost to regret or apprehension or high purpose. In the dark he could not stop from grinning because he was going up in an airplane.

The sky was lighter. Light seeped over the dry ground. East was pure gold. There was an airplane in it. They heard it first, a hornet droning up there. Then they saw it, turning, circling, coming down in its own noise. It bounced. It was down. It shook all over as its engines idled, the delicate, narrow, skyey thing—red, with silver wings.

A round door swung open and the pilot, with his ranger hat and his young brown face, looked out and said, "Morning, everybody. Come on, Henry. Show me your chart and let's get upstairs."

They shut him in the narrow glass dome in the seat behind the aviator's back. The plane shuddered, howled, rolled, bounced. Then it stopped, then it went on again, jarring his back teeth. The jarring stopped. They were climbing, spiraling up into the bright sky, soaring, in spite of machine noises, into a high peace.

The land was dark below them. "Can't see much yet,"

the man shouted. He swung north. Henry had the chart on his knees. They moved high over the northern edge of the park, where the thin line of the Tamiami Trail cut like a long thread straight from horizon to horizon. The sun that rose over the eastern clouds touched the earth down there with yellow light and he saw it was all brown, far to the north, far to the south.

"Saw grass," the aviator called. "Sweeps all the way down from Lake Okeechobee, curves southwest. The true 'glades." He took the plane around in a wide curve, in which the world tipped like water in a cup. When they were straight, he could look down and see every-where the tracks of paired wheels. "Froggers in 'glades buggies," the ranger shouted. "See the deer?" The plane slid down a long incline. Henry stared with delight down at the little, clear-cut, brown figures, like tiny toys. One stared up at them. One ran and stopped, bewildered at the noise. The plane soared upward. He could see long arms of dark green stretching among the brown grass below. Far away, the gulf was a veil of blue. He got the feeling of the vast low bulk of earth reaching far, far away, south and east, in the great familiar shape he re-membered from the map of Florida, the southmost land of the enormous country of the United States.

They overtook, down there, a great floating flock of white specks. "Egret and white ibis," the man said as Henry stared eagerly. The flock drifted and turned and floated over the mangroves, white petals floating in green hazy air like water. "Thousands of them," the voice said. "There's thousands more of them feeding down among the ponds and the trees. There's a rookery of white ibis. See? I don't want to buzz them. Makes them nervous."

It was an enormous bouquet of white flowers on a mound of green. "The young are just out of the egg. Those other flocks are going to the feeding ground."

The glass bumped Henry's nose as he looked down, holding his breath. It was amazing how plainly the whiteness of one single bird gleamed out, standing by a mud bank. He could not have counted them all. Eastward under the sun, the sheen of endless water high in the saw grass 'glades as far as he could see moved with them, like an old tarnished mirror scratched over with fine, fine lines of grass and little trees.

"Now Henry," the ranger shouted, "start watching your chart. See where we are? We're crossing all that open water at the head of the Broad River." Water flashed below. White birds by hundreds and hundreds rose as the sound of the plane trailed over them, flying lower. Mangrove and marsh and flashing ponds stretched westward. They crossed Broad Bay, then in another ten minutes, the width of Harney River.

"Got it?" the ranger shouted and Henry smiled back, "Yeah."

It was no longer, with him, the simple exhilaration of flight. His throat was tightening, his hands were moist. Now he was scared. Suppose he saw nothing?

Trees came up more distinctly. Ponds were bigger.

They were sliding lower. The world was nearer and bigger, coming up around them.

"Here's the Shark. There goes the Little Shark. Here's the branch—watch, Henry, watch.

His nose was glued to the glass. The plane curved a little, so that he looked almost straight down. They followed a gleam of water among trees, spreading water. He saw a pond. Was that the one? Did those dark trees cover the place where they had slept?

His heart nearly choked him, he was so sure. There was the place Dillon called "Alligator Crossing."

"A little more west," he yelled. The plane turned. He looked sharply down to the right. Below there, a great brown bird was moving. "See the eagle," he screamed, and pounded the man's back. "Is that an eagle tree?"

The aviator stared down on the right. "Sure is," he said.

But Henry was watching the left. It was there. He was sure it was, only a shadow under a tree by a bank—his throat closed. He could say nothing.

They flew on. After half an hour, Henry shouted, "I'd like to go back and look again, the way we've just come but farther west."

They turned. He was watching the land now below them, clutching the chart with fingers that shook, and staring.

The plane moved higher, circled, moved back again, in a long pattern of sweeping lines. They went south to Whitewater Bay, came back again. Henry looked down at the Labyrinth, where the water among the trees was cut into every kind of curvy shape, with no apparent beginning or ending. How anyone could ever get out of there . . . "Look, look," he shouted. "Go lower. I think I see the dinghy that I left."

Its tiny shape was plain, almost surrounded with mangroves. "Mark the chart," the aviator called. "Maybe we can figure some way to get it out of there. Boy, you sure were lost!"

But high again and going north the aviator called, "You don't see anything at all, Henry?"

Henry looked at the broad back before him. He had almost opened his mouth to shout. He had shown the aviator the eagle and the eagle tree to distract his attention and give himself time to think, because a new idea had suddenly come to him. If they found Dillon down there in the boat alive, they would find those alligator hides. They might put him in jail. They would certainly take his boat. And much as Henry hated him, he had also admired him, and he could not bear to do that.

"That's all," he shouted.

The aviator had his regular tour to finish. Perhaps, he reported, the man had got out after all, although he would go over the area again in the morning. All boats in the waterways should be checked by the rangers. If they found the man they would want to question him.

Henry sat rigid. They were ordered back to the landing, where a ranger waited for Henry. They watched the plane roar off and climb and turn. Ranger Brown said,

"Tough luck, Henry. But we won't give up yet. You're to stay with us for another day or more. We may want you for a witness. I guess you won't mind staying? You seem to take a lot of interest in things around here. Maybe you'll be a ranger one day."

It was a dazzling idea but Henry could only just manage a smile. He had something really serious to think out. For now that he knew Dillon's boat was still there where he had marked his chart with a thumbnail, he saw that it was up to him to get there first, and fast.

The End of the Search

THE old woman and the boy, in her small boat, had left the dock with the first light and were well down the coast when the sun was hot. In two hours of steady going they had found and turned into the mouth of Shark River. The sound of the engine echoed in the silence between the walls of mangrove, high and shadowy and remote.

Henry had told her why he had not known how he could get to Dillon's boat, even after he had seen clearly where it lay. The chart showed where that nameless branching river ran into the place where the Shark and the Little Shark divided. He remembered the confusion of streams and ponds through which Dillon had steered in order to get to the place he called "Alligator Crossing." Henry knew it would be easy for anyone else to take the wrong turn and get lost there again.

But what he had seen from the plane lay clearly defined on the chart. Across from Dillon's boat, under the great tree and up a bank, lay one of those stretches of dry ground and grass and scrub, like a deer meadow, that were often called "islands." There might be sloughs or wet places in it, but it seemed to extend from that bank west to the deeper stream. That was another branch of that unmarked river that ran into the Little Shark. He had marked it with his thumbnail. With her compass, he was certain, he could get across it on foot if she could put him ashore. Then she could go back and tell the rangers because he would have time enough to do what he had to do. The plane could hover over and show them the direct way to the boat.

If anything happened to him, he told her soberly, they'd know where to find him, too.

She had considered all that very carefully last night, studying his face as he talked with eyes no longer mild but sharp. At last she said, "All right, Henry. It's a good thing I have those extra cans of gas. I'll be glad to see you try it."

They had not spoken much in that two hours. He did not remember what he ate at breakfast. The little raccoon played about his feet. Sometimes he petted it. Most of the time he watched the coast or the river ahead.

Once, with his eyes absently on a kingfisher that was

clucking and flashing across the water just ahead, he said, "I suppose I'll have to get back next week to go to school." Then he looked at the machete beside him that he had sharpened again. It was nice the way the handle fitted his hand.

The outboard motor kept up its unchanging whine. Sometime later, not shifting her position from the tiller that, like Dillon, she could handle with an elbow, she shouted, "I've got to get to Miami in a week or two—to the dentist's. I stay at my sister's. Think you could come and see me?"

He nodded soberly at her. "I'd like to. If I could get there."

"We'll come and get you," she said. "I'd like to see your mother."

He considered this doubtfully, and said nothing.

Then she said, as if they had just been talking about it, "Yes, of course you have to go back to school. And I hope you won't be stupid about school, Henry. I suspect that you could learn a lot more in it if you thought that you could use it. And you can. I think those boys won't bother you so much now. You've grown bigger and heavier and I daresay you won't run away from them so much."

He considered that. To tell the truth, he not only felt bigger, he felt like an entirely different person.

She said then, "What are you going to do this summer?"

This summer? He looked blank. It was such a long time away that he had not thought about it at all.

"That's what I want to see your mother about," she said. "I want to take this boat around over to Miami and have it overhauled in my regular boatyard up the river. I'd like you to come over on the bus—I'll give you the money—to Everglades and help me take it around. We might as well go outside and have a good trip. Then I have to go north for a few weeks and I'd like you to live aboard and see to it that nothing happens. The boatyard man keeps the place locked, but you never can tell. Do you think you could do that?"

He stared at her as if he had not quite heard. Then he nodded with his eyes shining. All he could say now was, "Yes ma'am." He had to think about the chart folded in his lap. There was no way to tell which was the stream they wanted, until they found the place where the Little Shark branched off from the wider river.

Birds were going over by twos and threes, roused by the engine noise. "Wood ibis," she said. "Stork, you know." He followed the black tips on the great sailing wings, recognized the long, down-turned beak. Then a single bird flew right over the treetops, white with a sharp forked tail—a wonderful, easy, tumbling, stooping flight. "Fork-tailed kite," she shouted. "Wonderful bird. Look. He's got a tree snake dangling. Scooped it off a top branch. Watch him lift."

The stream that they followed widened; it was as blue ahead as the sky. To the left the mangroves thinned. They saw a greater stream going off. The place where it branched was wide and empty, lonely and aloof. The water pushed down steadily from the remote, hidden, watery 'glades at the heart of everything.

She brought the boat around in a wide circle, bouncing in its own chop. "There's your river then."

"It must be," he said.

It opened more narrowly to the south, often shadowed by the tallest mangroves he had ever seen, straight gray shafts springing up from the arches nearly seventy feet. Yet he couldn't be sure. He had seen so much. Except for their height and their color, the mangroves could have been all alike. Then, in an uproar that was its own echo, the boat came to the place where that stream branched.

Dillon had taken the narrower way more hidden with branches. Water from the other branch flowed smooth and silent and deep. They went that way now. The mangroves were shorter. There was more sun. There were muddy banks and willows, even palmetto heads rising tall, and bushes.

They went slowly. The river grew more shallow. Ahead, there were mudflats by the northern bank. Water came in from the west, enough to turn the boat in. This was the place.

They studied the chart. She stood up with the compass to set his course. To reach to the eastern side, where the boat lay as he had marked it, he must angle his way across north by east. She showed him the degree of the angle he must keep. At the other river, he might have to follow along the bank one way or other, but he must mark the place he came out, mark every step of the way with slashing the bushes, in order not to get lost.

"That's a lot of land to wander over," she told him. "You've got to be careful every minute."

He nodded at her. He had her canteen of water over a shoulder, wrapped sandwiches in his pocket, her compass slung around his neck, his machete in his hand. He picked up the little raccoon and dropped it on her knee. "Maybe you better ask the ranger to feed him until he can do for himself," he said. Then he got up on the bow and jumped to the bank. She waited until he waved to her and plunged rustling among the tall clumps of grass. Then she started the engine, backed to make the turn, and went off downstream. He heard the sharp engine noise grind away from him, growing smaller. At the last, the sound of it was lost in the noise of his own progress through dry weeds.

When he stopped first to check his line of march by the compass and found himself a mark in a palmetto up ahead, there was nothing around him in the sun but silence.

He had never before been aware of such silence. He found himself heeding the pulse in his own ears. An insect that he had passed began to chirp again, behind him. Somewhere far to his right a crow cawed. A leaf scratched on a bush in a bit of breeze. That was all.

He began walking as fast as he could, pushing through weeds and patches of rough earth. There were plumy tall grasses. He reached the palmetto and in its shade wiped the sweat from his face. It was hot. The ground was baked hot as if the sea winds could not get this far. He picked out another tree ahead on the compass line, a straggly red tree, and tramped toward it steadily. There was a tree snail above the crotch, a small yellow bubble of shell that made him grin. There were more trees and weeds and sun. Then an open place.

Trees were far away around him. Something tapped faintly on a branch and stopped. He felt the blood in his own ears. He had never been so alone in his life, in such silence. A kind of terror came to him, of aloneness. Whether he moved or stopped, it was heavy around him, heavy on his heart. He must go on. But he could feel how silence and aloneness might change a man, make him strange to himself. He wanted to move slowly, cautiously, make no sound. It made his feet heavy.

He had gone only a little way, he told himself, not half far enough. He must move faster. He set himself to briskness, humming a tune, slashing out with his machete at grass stems, at the low bushes. The sounds he made covered him. He reached another tree, another.

Suddenly he stopped. The silence was there, waiting for him. He looked slowly behind him. There was nothing there. If something had stood there, he could not have been more chilled. He walked again, so hard he was panting.

He was aware that where he walked probably no man

had ever gone before. He liked it, even as he was fearful. His heart pounded with excitement. He saw himself going forward across trackless wilderness, a small boy with knobby knees, sunburned, sunbleached, hatless, insignificant, alone. He was tall with pride.

But when something leaped heavily in the bushes to the left of him, crashed once, and was still, every nerve in his body jerked with the electricity of his fear.

He stood as still as a tree, holding his breath, staring. Then he was aware he was looking straight into round gold-and-black eyes, a tiger-colored head with tufted brown ears, a twitching nose. It hunched on a low branch and said "pah" to him silently, out of a pink gullet. It was a wildcat. It looked enormous to him but, because it had frightened him nearly to death, he ran at it swishing his machete and yelling, "Yah—ah—yah—yah!"

It leaped and vanished. And he went on again checking with his compass, jauntily enough. He had to skirt thorny bushes. He had to duck under branches. Sometimes the ground under his sneakers was quaking with wet and he had to jump from one grassy tussock to another.

He skirted a water hole and saw tracks in the mud, raccoon tracks, bird tracks, deer tracks. Sometimes he followed what he thought must be a deer path and it made him feel good. Once he saw the head of a deer feeding in the sunlit distance, the big white-lined ears twitching peacefully. Once he remembered that black bear they had released and how big he was. That was far away. But this would be a good place for bear, too, and curvy tan panthers with blunt cat noses.

It made no difference. He kept going. Once he sat under a tree and ate a sandwich and drank some water, one eye on his compass. He had come a long way.

When he got up to go on he realized how much time he had spent sitting in boats, not walking. His knees were stiff. His feet were too hot. His nose was sore with sun. It made no difference.

The thing was, he saw, to walk on steadily and carefully, not looking around too much, not thinking of silence and aloneness but of the compass line and of getting there.

He went through heavier trees, cutting his way—not mangroves, some gumbo-limbo, a rank growth. When he came out there was more wind blowing and the ground stretched open and weedy and shrubby, a long way ahead. He found a mark to work for and went forward, limping a little.

He was thinking of Dillon now and that was more frightening than anything. It made him walk faster because it seemed to him he could not wait any longer to find out how it was with him now, dead or alive.

So about the middle of the afternoon, startling a deer with a fawn and seeing some kind of a snake tail disappearing in grass to his right, seeing the eagle tree lift above to his left with the great nest in it, he came through bushes to the mud bank of the river he had been looking for. And he took a great breath.

He turned his head slowly to the right and there was the gray boat, under the dark arch of the tree. Everything was still.

As if he had walked so steadily all this time that he could not stop, he threw himself anyhow into the water, machete and all, thrashed and sputtered his way through it to the other side. When he touched mud he floundered up, hanging to the bank, and crawled along until his hand clutched the stern.

When he looked over into the cockpit Dillon was lying there, but not as he had been. He lay straight on his back, near the water bottle. Flies hung about him. There were bread papers around him and empty cans. He had a black stubble of beard on a face pasty white. As Henry looked, he moved a hand idly to shield his eyes. He was listening.

Henry's voice croaked. "Dillon."

The man turned his head a little and looked at him. He said huskily, "You been a long enough time getting here."

Henry climbed in and bent over him. "Are you—all right?"

"I'm near dead, for heaven's sake! I think my back is broke. I got so I could move a little. Where you been?"

"You want anything right now?" Henry said.

"Cup of coffee. Find me a cigarette."

Dripping, Henry plunged below. He wrenched the forward locker door open, reached in, and got the alligator hides. Counted them carefully. They made a big armload. He tossed them, one by one, up the bank.

Dillon said, "What you think you're doing? You crazy?"

Henry went over, gathered them up again, and carried them as far under the trees as he could go. He scratched a hole with the machete and buried them.

When he came back he stood over Dillon. "You got anything else on board they could put you in jail and take your boat away for?"

Dillon shook his head.

Henry found the matches, went ashore again, cut and broke a great heap of dry branches and grass piled on the open bank. When he scratched the match the yellow flame ran sputtering and pale in the sun. Dried leaves set up a great crackling fire and the smoke poured upward, white and gray, thin and hot. It went up higher and higher in a straight column until the wind caught it and bent it over, spreading it in a hazy fan that would creep along mile after mile. He piled on damp weeds. The smoke thickened. He knew just how it would look to a man in an airplane, circling even a long way off. Nothing of it was lost, a steady cloudy pillar. He thought how any minute now the squawk box on the ranger's boat, perhaps already far south of Lostman's, would be crackling with the aviator's rousing and directing voice.

Henry leaped aboard again and Dillon stared at him under his hand. "What you think you're up to now?" his puffed lips mumbled.

"Putting on water to boil," Henry said briskly. Nobody

could ever know, he thought, the weight that had lifted from his mind. Nobody could ever know what it had grown to be. "Coffee first," he said. "Then I figured I'd have time to kind of wash you up before they get here. Phew, you are dirty, you know."

"Don't touch me—let me alone—don't move me," the man said, and sweat broke out over his pasty face.

"I'll be careful. Honest," Henry said. He had a warm rag and soap and bent over him, gingerly. "Then I'll fix you some soup."

Dillon lay limp, his eyes closed, as if suddenly he gave up, no longer bracing himself to live somehow through those long nights and days. "You're—all right, Henry," he muttered. Henry began on his face, washing gently. It was funny that he had no particular emotion about the man anymore, certainly not bitterness or hatred. He admired his toughness and was grateful for it. But he had begun to see that you needed that, and a lot more, and something that was coming quietly to growth in him now, something that was—understanding, to get along in any man's world.

Author's Note

THE great south-pointing tip of the state of Florida,
the southernmost land on the mainland of the
United States, is probably the most unusual of all our
national parks. With the Ten Thousand Islands on the
lower west coast of Florida, it marks the end and delta
of the Everglades, the strangest river in the world.

A river of freshwater and of brown, sharp-edged saw
grass, it rises in the brimming water of Lake Okeechobee,
fed by rains and other rivers. Eighty miles wide, it forms
the central wilderness of south Florida, within the rocky
banks of the east and west coasts. Only its northern part,

*Editor's note: The information provided by the author here has not
been updated from its original, 1959 publication.*

by the lake, offers rich land for cultivation. Southward, the brown watery grass curves toward the west and makes the Everglades National Park. There, in a maze of watercourses and ponds, the saw grass gives way to the bewildering mangrove forests, rooted in brackish saltwater, which is one of the greatest concentrations of these remarkable trees in our hemisphere.

Down the width of the Everglades, shaped and pointed by the slow course of the surface freshwater during these thousands of years, crowd hundreds of tree-islands called "hammocks." They are like boats, like leafy mounds or small contained jungles that curve southwestward also. These are clumps of hardwoods growing out of rocky shapes—live oaks and willows in the north, and, in the south, palmettos, gumbo-limbos, black olives, some lovely small palms, cypresses, and even mahoganies. They are matted together with tough vines and are frowsy with air plants and orchids. About them the saw grass flows in its open, sun-blasted, riverlike plains.

Long before the retreating Seminole Indians found safety in the shadows of the northern hammocks, to which they paddled their shallow log canoes, and long before the first white men were on the coasts, an earlier race of Indians knew these saltwaters and these solitudes. With heavy conch shell picks they dug canals so that their canoes could go in shelter from one coast to another. They raised sand mounds out of high water for their village sites, burial mounds for their dead, and strangely shaped rows of mounds and causeways for their temples. New canals have been dug where the palmetto bulkheading still mark the outlines of these vanished, early-Indian canals. Mounds rise shadowy among the encroaching trees of hammocks and the shores of wandering west coast rivers.

Today the hammocks and grassy flats about them are the homes of deer and bear, panther, wildcat, raccoons, and opossum. Overhead, thousands and thousands of the amazing wading birds that fill the sunsets with the sound of their wings pass in flocks from their watery feeding grounds to the hammocks. Here, in their breeding season, they build their countless stick nests and rear their awkward, fuzzy-headed young. White egret, white ibis, blue and white heron, the enormous white pelicans that migrate here in winter, wood storks, the wonderful roseate spoonbills, smaller water birds in whirling hosts, water turkeys, wild turkeys, and all the migratory birds in their long flyways up and down the hemisphere make an unmatched spectacle.

The park area also includes much of the shallow, beautiful Bay of Florida that can be reached down the waterways from Miami, within the curve of the Upper Keys to the beaches of the mainland all the way around Cape Sable—the last of our continent. With Whitewater Bay within all that, and the wandering salty rivers and lagoons of the great mangrove wilderness, it is a marine park, known only to boats and filled with a shining diversity of fish that is available to sports fishermen and commercial fishermen within regulations.

Where the fishing village of Flamingo once straggled on the southern flats east of Cape Sable, the long road from Miami and Florida City ends in the pleasant building of the district park headquarters. There are restaurants, motels, campgrounds, and boat docks. The Coot Bay docks shelter boats available for the Whitewater Bay trips and fishing everywhere. On the west coast, the town of Everglades is the entrance to the western park area. The old fishing village of Chokoloskee and the islands and rivers are dominated by the Lostman's River Ranger Station of the Ten Thousand Islands.

The boundaries of the Everglades National Park, which in one place reaches to the Tamiami Trail, were at last defined in the spring of 1958. It was established first in 1947 when the State of Florida deeded one million of these strange acres to the Federal Department of the Interior and earmarked two million dollars for the purchase of additional land. Its total area is set now at 1,258,640 acres, of which a comparative few are reserved to private owners, so long as the land is used for farming.

The whole thing is an enormous, open, sunny wilderness of saw grass and fresh and saltwater, tree-islands and beaches—one of the youngest of all our national parks and the only tropical park on the mainland of the United States.

MARJORY STONEMAN DOUGLAS (1890–1998) lived in Florida for eighty-three years. One of Florida's foremost spokespersons for the environment, she was a journalist, writer of fiction and nonfiction, editor, publisher, and crusader for women's rights and racial justice. Her 1947 classic, *The Everglades: River of Grass,* focused the nation's conservation spirit on the Everglades region and continues to bring attention to this endangered area.

IF YOU ENJOYED THIS BOOK, YOU'LL ALSO WANT TO
READ THESE OTHER MILKWEED NOVELS.

*To order books or for more information, contact Milkweed at
(800) 520-6455 or visit our website (www.milkweed.org).*

THE $66 SUMMER
by John Armistead

MILKWEED PRIZE FOR CHILDREN'S LITERATURE
NEW YORK PUBLIC LIBRARY BEST BOOKS OF THE YEAR: "BOOKS FOR THE TEEN AGE"

By working at his grandmother's general store in Obadiah,
Alabama, during the summer of 1955, George Harrington figures he can save enough money to buy the motorcycle he wants, a
Harley-Davidson. Spending his off-hours with two friends, Esther
Garrison, fourteen, and Esther's younger brother, Bennett, the
unusual trio in 1950s Alabama—George is white and Esther and
Bennett are black—embark on a summer of adventure that turns
serious when they begin to uncover the truth about the racism in
their midst.

THE RETURN OF GABRIEL
by John Armistead

When Cooper Grant, Jubal Harris, and Squirrel Kogan form a
secret society called the Scorpions, they set their sights on getting
even with the school bully, Reno McCarthy. But it's 1964, and as
civil rights workers descend on their small Mississippi town and
the KKK gathers to respond, tension begins to rise. The boy's
camaraderie and courage are tested as each is swept up into the
tumultuous events of "Freedom Summer."

GILDAEN, THE HEROIC ADVENTURES OF A MOST UNUSUAL RABBIT
by Emilie Buchwald

CHICAGO TRIBUNE BOOK FESTIVAL AWARD, BEST BOOK FOR AGES 9–12

Gildaen is befriended by a mysterious being who has lost his memory but not the ability to change shape at will. Together they accept the perilous task of thwarting the evil sorcerer, Grimald, in this tale of magic, villainy, and heroism.

THE OCEAN WITHIN
by V. M. Caldwell

MILKWEED PRIZE FOR CHILDREN'S LITERATURE

Elizabeth is a foster child who has just been placed with the boisterous and affectionate Sheridans, a family that wants to adopt her. Accustomed to having to fend for herself, however, Elizabeth is reluctant to open up to them. During a summer spent by the ocean with the eight Sheridan children and their grandmother, dubbed by Elizabeth as "Iron Woman" because of her strict discipline, Elizabeth learns what it means—and how much she must risk—to become a permanent member of a loving family.

TIDES
by V. M. Caldwell

Recently adopted twelve-year-old Elizabeth Sheridan is looking forward to spending the summer at Grandma's oceanside home. But on her stay there, she faces problems involving her cousins, five-year-old Petey and eighteen-year-old Adam, that cause her to question whether the family will hold together. As she and Grandma help each other through troubling times, Elizabeth comes to see that she has become an important member of the family.

Parents Wanted
by George Harrar

MILKWEED PRIZE FOR CHILDREN'S LITERATURE

After five "adoption parties" and no luck, Andy Fleck, the kid nobody wanted, faces his biggest challenge yet—learning how to live with parents who seem to love him. Placed in a new foster home with Jeff and Laurie, he has a chance to get out of the grip of his past, which includes a jailed father and a mother who gave him up to the state. But Andy can't keep himself from challenging every limit that his foster parents set. So far, Laurie and Jeff have refused to give up on their difficult new charge. But will he go too far?

No Place
by Kay Haugaard

Arturo Morales and his fellow sixth-grade classmates decide to improve their neighborhood and their lives by building a park in their otherwise concrete, inner-city Los Angeles barrio. The kids are challenged by their teachers to figure out what it would take to transform the neighborhood junkyard into a clean, safe place for children to play. Despite their parents' skepticism and the threat of street gangs, Arturo and his classmates struggle to prove that the actions of individuals—even kids—can make a difference.

The Monkey Thief
by Aileen Kilgore Henderson

NEW YORK PUBLIC LIBRARY BEST BOOKS OF THE YEAR: "BOOKS FOR THE TEEN AGE"

Twelve-year-old Steve Hanson is sent to Costa Rica for eight months to live with his uncle. There he discovers a world completely unlike anything he can see from the cushions of his couch back home, a world filled with giant trees and insects, mysterious sounds, and the constant companionship of monkeys swinging in the branches overhead. When Steve hatches a plan to capture a monkey for himself, his quest for a pet leads him into dangerous territory. It takes all of Steve's survival skills—and the help of his new friends—to get him out of trouble.

THE SUMMER OF THE BONEPILE MONSTER
by Aileen Kilgore Henderson

MILKWEED PRIZE FOR CHILDREN'S LITERATURE
ALABAMA LIBRARY ASSOCIATION 1996 JUVENILE/YOUNG ADULT AWARD
MAUDE HART LOVELACE AWARD FINALIST

Eleven-year-old Hollis Orr has been sent to spend the summer with Grancy, his father's grandmother, in rural Dolliver, Alabama, while his parents "work things out." As summer begins, Hollis encounters a road called Bonepile Hollow, barred by a gate and a real skull and crossbones mounted on a board. "Things that go down that road don't ever come back," he is told. Thus begins the mystery that plunges Hollis into real danger.

TREASURE OF PANTHER PEAK
by Aileen Kilgore Henderson

NEW YORK PUBLIC LIBRARY BEST BOOKS OF THE YEAR: "BOOKS FOR THE TEEN AGE"

Twelve-year-old Page Williams begrudgingly accompanies her mother, Ellie, as she flees her abusive husband, Page's father. Together they settle in a fantastic new world—Big Bend National Park, Texas. Wild animals stalk through the park, and the nearby Ghost Mountains are filled with legends of lost treasures. As Page tests her limits by sneaking into forbidden canyons, Ellie struggles to win the trust of other parents. Only through their newfound courage are they able to discover a treasure beyond what they could have imagined.

I Am Lavina Cumming
by Susan Lowell

In 1905, ten-year-old Lavina is sent from her home on the Bosque Ranch in Arizona Territory to live with her aunt in the city of Santa Cruz, California. Armed with the Cumming family motto, "courage," Lavina deals with a new school, homesickness, a very spoiled cousin, an earthquake, and a big decision about her future.

The Boy with Paper Wings
by Susan Lowell

Confined to bed with a viral fever, eleven-year-old Paul sails a paper airplane into his closet and propels himself into mysterious and dangerous realms in this exciting and fantastical adventure. Paul finds himself trapped in the military diorama on his closet floor, out to stop the evil commander, KRON. Armed only with paper and the knowledge of how to fold it, Paul uses his imagination and courage to find his way out of dilemmas and disasters.

The Secret of the Ruby Ring
by Yvonne MacGrory

Lucy gets a very special birthday present, a star ruby ring, from her grandmother and finds herself transported to Langley Castle in the Ireland of 1885. At first, she is intrigued by castle life, in which she is the lowliest servant, until she loses the ruby ring and her only way home.

EMMA AND THE RUBY RING
by Yvonne MacGrory

Only one day short of her eleventh birthday and looking forward
to spending time with her dad, Emma wakes up not at her cousin
Lucy's, where she has been visiting, but in a nineteenth-century
Irish workhouse. Emma learns that the ruby ring can grant two
wishes to its wearer, and now, at a time of dire historical unrest,
she must prove she can be the heroic girl she wants to be.

A BRIDE FOR ANNA'S PAPA
by Isabel R. Marvin

MILKWEED PRIZE FOR CHILDREN'S LITERATURE

Life on Minnesota's iron range in 1907 is not easy for thirteen-
year-old Anna Kallio. Her mother's death has left Anna to take
care of the house, her young brother, and her father, a black-
smith in the dangerous iron mines. So she and her brother plot
to find their father a new wife, even attempting to arrange a
match with one of the "mail order" brides arriving from Finland.

MINNIE
by Annie M. G. Schmidt

WINNER OF THE NETHERLANDS' SILVER PENCIL PRIZE AS ONE OF THE
BEST BOOKS OF THE YEAR

Miss Minnie is a cat. Or rather, she *was* a cat. She is now a human,
and she's not at all happy to be one. As Minnie tries to find and
reverse the cause of her transformation, she brings her reporter
friend, Mr. Tibbs, news from the cats' gossip hotline—including
revealing information that one of the town's most prominent citi-
zens is not the animal lover he appears to be.

THE DOG WITH GOLDEN EYES
by Frances Wilbur

MILKWEED PRIZE FOR CHILDREN'S LITERATURE
TEXAS LONE STAR READING LIST

Many girls dream of owning a dog of their own, but Cassie's wish for one takes an unexpected turn in this contemporary tale of friendship and growing up. Thirteen-year-old Cassie is lonely, bored, and feeling friendless when a large, beautiful dog appears one day in her suburban backyard. Cassie wants to adopt the dog, but as she learns more about him, she realizes that she is, in fact, caring for a full-grown Arctic wolf. As she attempts to protect the wolf from urban dangers, Cassie discovers that she possesses strengths and resources she never imagined.

BEHIND THE BEDROOM WALL
by Laura E. Williams

MILKWEED PRIZE FOR CHILDREN'S LITERATURE
NEW YORK PUBLIC LIBRARY BEST BOOKS OF THE YEAR: "BOOKS FOR THE TEEN AGE"
MAUDE HART LOVELACE AWARD FINALIST
SUNSHINE STATE YOUNG READER'S AWARD MASTER LIST
JANE ADDAMS PEACE AWARD HONOR BOOK

It is 1942. Thirteen-year-old Korinna Rehme is an active member of her local *Jungmädel*, a Nazi youth group, along with many of her friends. Korinna's parents, however, secretly are members of an underground group providing a means of escape to the Jews of their city and are, in fact, hiding a refugee family behind the wall of Korinna's bedroom. As Korinna comes to know the family, especially their young daughter, her sympathies begin to turn. But when someone tips off the Gestapo, loyalties are put to the test and Korinna must decide in what she believes and whom she trusts.

THE SPIDER'S WEB
by Laura E. Williams

Thirteen-year-old Lexi Jordan has just joined the Pack, a group of
neo-Nazi skinheads, as a substitute for the close-knit family she
wishes she had. After she and the Pack spray paint a synagogue,
Lexi hides from her pursuers on the front porch of elderly
Ursula Zeidler's home, a former member of the Hitler Youth
Group, who painfully recalls her ugly anti-Semitic Nazi activities
and betrayal of a friend. When her younger sister becomes en-
thralled with Lexi's new "family," Lexi realizes the true meaning
of the Pack and has little time to save herself and her sister from
its sinister grip.

MILKWEED EDITIONS publishes with the intention of making a humane impact on society, in the belief that literature is a transformative art uniquely able to convey the essential experiences of the human heart and spirit. To that end, Milkweed publishes distinctive voices of literary merit in handsomely designed, visually dynamic books, exploring the ethical, cultural, and esthetic issues that free societies need continually to address. Milkweed Editions is a not-for-profit press.

JOIN US

Since its genesis as *Milkweed Chronicle* in 1979, Milkweed has helped hundreds of emerging writers reach their readers. Thanks to the generosity of foundations and of individuals like you, Milkweed Editions is able to continue its nonprofit mission of publishing books chosen on the basis of literary merit—of how they impact the human heart and spirit—rather than on how they impact the bottom line. That's a miracle our readers have made possible.

In addition to purchasing Milkweed books, you can join the growing community of Milkweed supporters. Individual contributions of any amount are both meaningful and welcome. Contact us for a Milkweed catalog or log on to www.milkweed.org and click on "About Milkweed," then "Why Join Milkweed," to find out about our donor program, or simply call (800) 520-6455 and ask about becoming one of Milkweed's contributors. As a nonprofit press, Milkweed belongs to you, the community. Milkweed's board, its staff, and especially the authors whose careers you help launch thank you for reading our books and supporting our mission in any way you can.

Interior design by Christian Fünfhausen
Typeset in New Baskerville 10.5/15
by Stanton Publication Services.
Printed on acid-free, recycled 55# Natural
Odyssey Hibulk paper
by Friesen Corporation.